Dear Santa,

I've been a good boy all year.

The reason I'm writing is to let you know we moved after my dad died. We're in Montana now. Me and my sister like it here. There's bugs all over and rabbits and snakes. My mom is scared of the snakes.

That's why I need a cowboy outfit for Christmas, like the kind Zach "Lightning" Lucas wears. If I had one, I could rope some rabbits and shoot the snakes so my mom wouldn't be scared.

I know about money and how there's not much around, so if a cowboy outfit is too expensive, maybe you could send a real cowboy instead. Then my mom wouldn't be scared of nothing.

Thanks,

Andy Collins

P.S. My sister wants one of those princess crowns with jewels on it.

**Books by Janet Tronstad**

Love Inspired

*An Angel for Dry Creek
*A Gentleman for Dry Creek
*A Bride for Dry Creek
*A Rich Man for Dry Creek
*A Hero for Dry Creek
*A Baby for Dry Creek
*A Dry Creek Christmas
*Sugar Plums for Dry Creek
*At Home in Dry Creek
**The Sisterhood of the Dropped Stitches
*A Match Made in Dry Creek
*Shepherds Abiding in Dry Creek
**A Dropped Stitches Christmas
*Dry Creek Sweethearts
**A Heart for the Dropped Stitches
*A Dry Creek Courtship
*Snowbound in Dry Creek

*Dry Creek
**The Sisterhood of the Dropped Stitches

Steeple Hill Single Title

*Going to the Chapel*

## JANET TRONSTAD

grew up on a small farm in central Montana. One of her favorite things to do was to visit her grandfather's bookshelves, where he had a large collection of Zane Grey novels. She's always loved a good story. Today, Janet lives in Pasadena, California, where she is a full-time writer.

# Snowbound in Dry Creek
## Janet Tronstad

Refreshed version of
STRANDED WITH SANTA,
revised by author

Steeple
Hill®

Published by Steeple Hill Books™

STEEPLE HILL BOOKS

Steeple
Hill®

ISBN-13: 978-0-373-81379-7
ISBN-10:    0-373-81379-1

SNOWBOUND IN DRY CREEK

This is the revised text of the work which was first published as
*Stranded with Santa* by Harlequin Enterprises Limited in 2002.

Copyright © 2002 by Janet Tronstad

Revised text copyright © 2008 by Janet Tronstad

This edition published by arrangement with Steeple Hill Books.

® and TM are trademarks of Steeple Hill Books, used under license.
Trademarks indicated with ® are registered in the United States Patent
and Trademark Office, the Canadian Trade Marks Office and in other
countries.

www.SteepleHill.com

**Printed in U.S.A.**

And the angel said unto them, Fear not: for, behold, I bring you good tidings of great joy, which shall be to all people. For unto you is born this day in the city of David a Savior, which is Christ the Lord.

—*Luke* 2:10–11

This book is dedicated with love
to my good friend, Darlene Hanson.
She is a warm-hearted woman with lots of class.

# *Chapter One*

The last thing Jenny Collins needed was rain on her windshield, especially since her old car had just hissed and then died in the middle of what was clearly the only street in this postage-stamp of a town. She and her children had begun this move to Dry Creek, Montana, with high hopes, but their enthusiasm had deserted them a thousand miles back down the road.

It was the middle of the afternoon and the day itself was gloomy. There wasn't another car in sight except for the ones parked beside the road.

"The car stopped," eight-year-old Lisa announced calmly as though her mother might not have noticed.

"I know, dear."

"I don't like the rain."

"I know that, too, dear."

Jenny had figured there was no point in packing their old, beat-up umbrella. By spring, she would have a job and could buy an umbrella that actually stayed open without someone's thumb constantly pressing on the button at the bottom of the rod. So she threw the broken one away.

And now, suddenly, it was clear she'd made a mistake. The lack of that old umbrella seemed to symbolize Jenny's whole disastrous plan. She hadn't thought things through. In her first rush of enthusiasm, she'd told herself that their move to Dry Creek would be a shining example to her children of the way God was taking care of them after their father had died. But after the car's muffler gave out in Nevada and the radiator overheated in Utah, she had no longer been able to convince herself that anything was going as it should. And now she hadn't even got the umbrella right.

"It'll be fine," Jenny said for the sake of her children. She prayed that she was right.

She had started to wonder in Idaho if she'd misunderstood God. Maybe what she thought was God's provision for them was nothing more than a widow's foolish dream. She knew why she thought the move here would be good, but maybe

God didn't agree. Even though she had given up on Stephen's love for *her* long before he died, she refused to give up on it for their children. She didn't want them to think that their father hadn't cared enough to make any kind of a plan for them when he knew he was dying.

The old farm that Stephen had inherited from his uncle was really all they had left after Jenny had settled their debts in Los Angeles, so she finally decided in her own mind that it was Stephen's final gift to their children—a gift she wanted them to experience to the fullest. She believed all children needed something from their fathers, and her children would have this farm and the knowledge that their father had spent many summers on it as a boy. In time, she hoped the farm itself would look like evidence of Stephen's concern for them.

"Don't worry. We're almost there." Jenny pushed her thoughts aside and kept her voice upbeat. She looked back and smiled at her children. Lisa was strapped into the middle of the backseat and four-year-old Andy was in his car seat to her right. The rest of the backseat, like the trunk, was filled with their belongings. "We'll be warm and dry in no time at all when we get to your father's farm."

Lisa looked at her.

"We'll get the car going again soon, too," Jenny assured her daughter as she slipped the key out of the ignition. "It's probably nothing serious. But we need to stop and ask directions to our place before we go farther, anyway. These people might have known your father when he was a boy. Imagine that."

Lisa didn't say anything.

It worried Jenny that neither Lisa nor Andy had said anything about their father after he died. Was that normal?

"There's no school here." Lisa craned her neck to look out the side window. "If there's no school, I'm going back home."

Home to Lisa was their old apartment in El Monte, southeast of Los Angeles. They'd moved into that run-down two-bedroom apartment a year and a half ago. Jenny had thought at the time that it was as low as their little family could go. She'd been wrong. What she had seen as temporary housing until Stephen was able to work again turned into an apartment she tried, and failed, to keep after he died.

Her receptionist job hadn't paid much even before her hours were cut back. Stephen had been dead for six months by then. That's when she'd decided God must want them to move to Dry Creek. The farm was all they had left. Even with her doubts now, she couldn't think of any other options they might have had. If they'd stayed in Los Angeles, they would have needed to move into a hotel room. Apartment rents were too high, but some of the older hotels rented rooms by the week.

Jenny didn't want her children to grow up in a hotel room. Not when there was a choice.

"There has to be a school someplace," Jenny answered as she, too, took a better look out of the windows. It was raining harder by now, but she could still see the buildings. There was a church; she could identify the white frame structure by the steeple on top of it. There were a dozen or so houses, all of them obviously occupied either because of their porch lights or the dogs in their yards.

But Lisa was right; there was no school. No library, either, and Lisa loved to read. Jenny supposed it was too much to hope that they had a ballet class anywhere within fifty miles of here. Jenny loved to wear her pink tutu and pretend she was a princess.

Jenny hadn't expected Dry Creek to be quite so small. The only building that looked like it might belong in a bigger town was the café. She would have taken the children over there instead of bracing herself to go into the building straight ahead except for the fact that a café usually meant money and she didn't want to part with any more of hers than was necessary. Besides, they still had some apples and cheese in their cooler, and she could heat up a can of soup when they got to the farm.

No, the other building was better for what she needed. If the sign over its door were to be believed, it was a hardware store. Surely, the children wouldn't want anything from the shelves of a hardware store.

"There's Thunder," Andy said, with reverence in his voice, as he pointed to a sign she hadn't noticed on the side of the store. It advertised some brand of animal feed and, sure enough, there was a black horse staring right at them.

The two heroes in Andy's young life were the cowboy Zach "Lightning" Lucas and the man's faithful black horse, Thunder. Pictures of the two of them were always on the box of Ranger Flakes, Andy's favorite breakfast cereal.

"It's a different horse, sweetie," Jenny said before Andy could ask if they were finally going to meet his idols. Andy was so awestruck by them he had even started mentioning the cowboy and horse in his evening prayers. Jenny hoped there were some young boys around here who could be Andy's friends. If he had more flesh-and-blood people in his life, maybe he would give up the cardboard ones.

At least Andy had been happy to leave Los Angeles once she'd told him there were cowboys and horses in Montana. Jenny only wished Lisa had something like that to make the move easier for her. Unfortunately, the street outside didn't have anything a princess would like.

Jenny took a last look at the afternoon sky. It was getting darker. "Put your coats on and we'll go inside the store."

The only things she'd bought before she left Los Angeles were two heavy coats for the children. She might not have an umbrella, but she was ready for snow. That should count for something. Jenny reached behind her and pulled the flannel shirt off the seat. She'd wrap that around herself.

"Careful of the mud," Jenny said as she opened the car door. "And wait for me on the porch."

They all ran as quickly as they could and stood a minute under the overhang that sheltered the porch. Jenny could hear the rain beating on the roof. She took a deep breath and then opened the door.

Warm air pushed at her as she stood in the doorway. She smelled stale coffee and burning wood. Lisa was a little in front of her and Andy was to the side. Both children were wide-eyed as they looked around. Jenny didn't blame them; she'd never seen a store like this in her entire life, either. There were the usual shelves of things for sale, like bins of nails and brooms and shovels. But that's where everything normal stopped.

In the middle of the plain oak floor there was a potbelly wood stove that had a couple of old men sitting around it with their boots off and their stocking feet stretched out to the stove's warmth.

"Well, it's not the same thing for all women," one of the men protested loudly. He obviously hadn't heard Jenny and the children enter the store. "Every woman is looking for something different in a husband. Just like horses with their feed. They're particular."

The other old man snorted. "And you just happen to know what that something different is?"

The first one reared back. "That's what I've been sitting here telling you for the past half hour."

Jenny almost felt as if she should clear her

throat to let the men know someone was there.
Then she remembered how cold it was outside
and closed the door behind the children. The
door gave a loud click as she shut it. That was
as good as clearing her throat. By the time she
turned around, the men were all looking at her
and the children.

"Good. Here's a woman," the first man said.
"We'll ask her. Then you'll see what I mean."

"I'm afraid we're just here for directions,"
Jenny mumbled. Lisa and Andy were already
walking toward the fire's warmth. She couldn't
blame them; they'd all gotten damp in the rain.

Neither man looked as if they were listening to Jenny.

"Okay, prove it," the second man finally said.
He pointed at Jenny. "You tell me what she wants
from a husband and we'll see if you're right."

"It would be my pleasure," the first man said
with a smile in Jenny's direction. "Elmer
Maynard at your service, ma'am. Now, if I
may—"

"Charley Nelson, here." The other man
nodded at Jenny.

"I really don't think—"

Elmer had his eyes closed and a deep frown
on his face. "Now a woman like her—" he
managed to point at Jenny even with his eyes

still closed "—she's apt to want a man who's good with children."

The other man, Charley, barked out a quick laugh. "Well, any fool can see that. The kids are sitting right here in front of us. Obviously, she wanted kids."

Lisa and Andy had been given prime seats next to the woodstove and they were watching the old men as if they were in the middle of a *Sesame Street* episode.

"I'm just getting started." Elmer opened his eyes and glared at the other man. "She probably also wanted a husband who was athletic, someone who would be a good father and play catch with her son—"

Elmer stopped to smile down at Andy. Jenny figured it was a kindly gesture, but it was also the older man's fatal mistake. Andy had a one-track mind these days.

"Ohhh, could he be a cowboy?" Andy asked breathlessly, his eyes wide with hope as he looked up at the older man. "With a black horse?"

Andy wiggled as though he was suddenly overcome with the possibilities and then he continued in a low whisper. "Could it be Zach Lightning Lucas?"

"Who's that?" Elmer turned to Jenny with puzzled eyes.

"You'd have to eat cold cereal to know," Jenny said with a smile. "He's just some guy pretending to be a rodeo star."

"Well, tell your husband not to worry then. All boys like cowboys when they're little like this. I would have traded my father for the Lone Ranger when I was this little guy's age. But we all grow out of it. What does your husband do, anyway?"

Jenny stood up. "Nothing."

"Well, I'm sure he'll find work," Elmer said as he smoothed back his hair. "Tell him not to lose hope."

"He doesn't need hope, he's dead."

"Oh," Charley said in dismay.

"Oh," Elmer echoed in shock.

Jenny wished she'd worked up to that revelation. She'd let her unease with the conversation come between her and these new neighbors.

"Well—" Charley mumbled.

Elmer cleared his throat.

"It's been a while since he died," Jenny added flatly. She didn't need any words of sympathy. "We're fine. We just stopped in to get directions to a farm he inherited. I'm sorry, but I don't really need a husband."

"Well, but surely a husband—" Elmer started to say before Charley gave him a fierce look.

"Don't pay him any attention," Charley said quietly to Jenny. "We believe in minding our own business here in Dry Creek. Elmer's just trying to prove he's a matchmaker. Next month he'll be back to worrying about what color of blue to paint his Cadillac."

"Well, I'm sure other women will be happy if he finds them a husband," Jenny said politely. "But all I need is directions."

"Of course," Charley said as he reached into his shirt pocket and drew out a small stub of a pencil. "If the place is around here, we can tell you how to get there. I'll even draw you a map. I'm getting pretty good at maps now that I'm the relief mail driver. I know the quickest way to every place."

Meanwhile, Elmer reached into the top pocket in his bib overalls. "Anyone want some candy?"

Jenny recognized the gesture as a peace offering and nodded to Andy and Lisa, letting them know they could each take one of the wrapped chocolates the man held in the palm of his hand. She wanted to be friendly to the first people she met in the area. After all, these men would be their neighbors.

By the time the men had drawn a rough map showing her how to get to their property, Jenny was beginning to feel more optimistic about settling in this community. They all remembered little Stephen Collins who had visited his uncle every summer for years.

The fact that the men seemed to have fond memories of her late husband gave Jenny the courage to mention that her car had stalled out front in the middle of the road. The men had to walk to the window to look, and they seemed to agree that the car was in trouble. She asked for the number to call a tow truck operator, but the men waved that idea away. The nearest tow truck, they said, was in Miles City, and the way business was backed up there it would take twenty-four hours before it'd come to Dry Creek.

Instead, Charley offered to help get the car started and then follow her out to the Collins farm, just to be sure they all got there in one piece, he said. Jenny and the children walked with him out to the porch.

"Are you always this kind to strangers?" Jenny asked Charley.

"You betcha," Charley said with a nod and a grin. "We make it a policy around here."

He had their car running in twenty minutes.

Four weeks later, Zach "Lightning" Lucas stood on the same weathered porch and scowled as the same gray sky darkened. "Whatever happened to that small-town hospitality I've heard about? You know, that kindness to strangers thing?"

"What about it?" Charley shrugged as he cheerfully slipped another handful of candy canes into the mail bag Zach had slung over his shoulder. "You're able-bodied."

"Don't you require people to pass some test if you want them to deliver your mail?"

"We had the foresight to have people sign forms saying that, in an emergency, civilians could carry their mail. Today, that would be you."

Zach grunted. At least the man realized a sick horse was an emergency. Charley was apparently the closest thing to a vet in this small town and he'd agreed to treat Zach's horse, Thunder.

The two men were far enough down on the porch that Zach could look into the window of the hardware store and see a group of old men sitting around that potbelly stove. Fortunately, older men like these tended to eat oatmeal instead of cold cereal, and none of them had recognized him or Thunder. Of course, they might have treated them with more respect if they had.

When he first stepped inside the store, Zach hadn't even gotten his piece said before those old men were asking him if he was a single man. They got that one question out there faster than most women did in the pick-up bars down in the panhandle. And those women prided themselves on being brazen. Zach knew it was true from experience.

Zach told the men he didn't need any help with his love life; he had a sick horse.

At the mention of Thunder, Charley had sat up straight and paid attention. It had taken a few minutes, but finally Zach had laid out his problem. His sick horse had to have veterinary care as soon as possible.

Charley was willing to tend the horse, and the other men all agreed he was the closest thing to a vet this small town had, so Zach relaxed. That is, until he realized that Charley had a problem of his own. It seemed Charley was the relief mail carrier, as well, and needed to deliver the mail one last time before Christmas. If Charley was going to tend Thunder, someone else needed to take around the mail.

Zach hadn't realized it was December 23rd already, but he figured the date didn't mean too much. Charley asked for a volunteer to deliver the mail, and not a man inside the store had done anything except stare at the floor like he was suddenly deaf. Zach thought maybe there was a lot of heavy lifting because of last-minute packages or something.

Well, he could understand that. If those boxes were heavy, he wouldn't want any of these older men to strain their back muscles. Having a bad back might interfere with them sitting there and harassing strangers.

So Zach volunteered. He said he'd be happy to help out. How hard could it be to toss around a few boxes? He was in prime lifting shape.

Zach couldn't help but notice that he'd barely got his offer out before the men sitting around the stove started grinning like a bunch of renegade dogs that had trapped an unsuspecting cat.

Five minutes later, Zach was standing on the porch and he understood why the men were so full of glee. Charley had promised the regular mail carrier that he'd deliver the mail the way she always did on the last day before Christmas. She, a Mrs. Brown, always made it look like Santa was out there delivering the letters himself on that day.

Zach figured Charley would have offered to treat a rabid skunk if it meant he could convince someone else to take his place on this particular mail run.

Zach pushed his Stetson hat lower on his head. He didn't know anyone in this crazy one-stop town, but he still didn't like the men looking at him from inside that store. Suppose one of them recognized him even now. He was Zach "Lightning" Lucas and he had a reputation to uphold—a reputation that didn't include a fuzzy red fat-suit and a black plastic belt. It was bad enough that the four-wheel drive postal truck had a fake set of reindeer horns tied to the grill and a ball of mistletoe swinging from the antenna. He didn't need Christmas fuzz all over himself, too.

Zach grimaced as red and green flashes met his eyes. The lightbulbs hanging from the reindeer horns were on a timer. When he first saw them, he'd hoped they were merely ornamental. No such luck. The men inside the store had all come to the window to see the show when he'd tried out the lights. If it hadn't been for all of the green lights flashing, they would have thought the town was on fire because of all the red lights flashing.

Zach didn't know how much holiday nonsense he could take. He just wasn't a Christmas kind of a guy. After all, he had more gold-plated champion belt buckles than most men had ties. He had fans who knew his name—lots of fans since he'd endorsed that Ranger breakfast cereal. Those fans obviously didn't live in Dry Creek, but people in many other towns recognized him in grocery stores and in laundromats. He was Zach "Lightning" Lucas. He was *famous*. He was entitled to some dignity.

Unfortunately, Zach had a feeling his dignity was about to be covered in padding and thoroughly ignored for the day.

And it was all because of Christmas. Not that Zach should be surprised. Christmas had been giving him trouble for years. It always depressed him with all that family stuff. Not that he had anything against families—it's just that family stuff wasn't for a man like him.

That's why, this year, he had made a plan. He should have thought to tell the men inside the store that he had his own way of dealing with love during the holidays.

Zach and Thunder were only passing through Montana, heading over to Interstate 15 for the long stretch down to Las Vegas. Once there, Thunder would board at a ranch some miles outside of Vegas while Zach hit the Strip. The neon lights and showgirls—well, if her return message were to be believed, one showgirl in particular—would make him forget the holidays were even here.

He and Thunder had been making good time,

too, Zach thought mournfully, until the horse got a fever.

"You've got the map." Charley patted his pockets as though the slip of paper showing all the county roads might still be there instead of taped to the dashboard of the postal truck.

"Yes, sir."

The winter air had a bite to it, but Zach was in no hurry to leave the porch and get into that decked-out postal truck. He might as well ride around in a clown's cart and be done with it. Which made him think of something.

"I can't be driving the postal truck," Zach said. "Isn't that against some kind of a law? Government property and all."

"The thing belongs to Dry Creek, so it's not postal property. We got it in some sale last year. Rural carriers out here aren't generally issued postal vehicles."

"Well, then, I'd be glad to drive my truck," Zach said.

"Don't have time for that. I can't pull your horse trailer with my pickup. So I need to drive your truck if you want your horse to get into the barn before the snow gets any worse."

Zach hung his head. He couldn't be choosy, not when Thunder needed help.

Both men were silent for a moment.

"Well then, let me get that apple pie my fiancée, Edith, baked for the Collins family." Charley said as he stepped back and opened the door of the store. He reached inside to pick up something sitting on a chair by the door. It was a foil-wrapped package. "Remember that name—Collins. That'll be the last stop on your list. And the box in back is for them, too. Their car is broken. Radiator. So Edith said she'd pick up some things for them and send them out in the mail truck." Charley lifted the pie. "There's two of the cutest kids you'll ever meet out there."

Zach nodded. He'd already met every kid on the planet—both the cute and the ugly. The ones he missed at the rodeos he met because they ate Ranger Flakes breakfast cereal. Not that he was complaining. He liked kids better than he liked most adults. He did glance over at the window of the hardware store though. Apparently, the men had got tired of laughing at him and gone back to sit by the fire. They were probably deciding who to torture next.

Charley smiled and looked at Zach slyly. "'Course, one look at their mother and you'll see why they're so cute."

Zach grunted as he turned back to the old man. Now that was the part of meeting kids he didn't like—their mothers. Even the women who were married always seemed to have a scheme to get him married off to someone. You'd think there was something wrong with a man choosing to live in hotel rooms and wash his socks in bathroom sinks.

Charley must have known what he was thinking because he shook his head. "The poor woman. Such a pity—"

Charley looked at Zach as though he expected some curiosity.

Zach had none.

Charley ploughed ahead, anyway. "Jenny Collins is a widow. Not that she's old, mind you. No, sir. Moved up here a couple of weeks ago—surprised us all. She'd been married to Jeb Collins's nephew." Charley nodded at Zach as though Zach had known this Jeb, whoever he was. "Jeb had left the place to his nephew, but we all thought the nephew would have sense enough to sell it before he started dying of that cancer of his. But he didn't. Stephen was his name. Don't know what he was thinking. Surely he didn't expect his widow to move up here with the two kids. What do you think a city woman's gonna do with a place like that, anyway?"

Zach shrugged. He didn't like to get involved in the problems of strangers.

Charley had no such hesitation. "I hear she's been getting magazines on farm management!" He shook his head. "She's a game one, I'll give her that. She had so many questions, Edith gave her an old guide book on living in Montana. But it's no place for her and the kids—even old man Collins used to move into town here for the winter months. The house doesn't even have a decent road leading up to it. Ruts a mile deep, and it drifts closed every time there's a blizzard."

Charley took a breath before he continued. "The regular mail carrier, you know, the Delores Brown I told you about, always drives the mail right up to the house for the Collins family. But with the next hard snow they won't get mail for a week. The county snowplow doesn't go that far out. Most farmers out that way have plows on their tractors or something. But all the woman's got is that car of hers—and with the two little ones—well, Edith is worried about their car not working."

Between Edith Hargrove and Delores Brown, Zach had already concluded, the two women pretty well worried about everything and everybody within a hundred-mile radius. He was surprised they didn't go into politics. They could form their own party.

Charley stopped suddenly and squinted at Zach. "What Jenny Collins needs is a husband."

Zach looked at the other man in amazement and then pushed his hat farther down on his head. "Don't look at me. I'm just trying to get my horse fixed up. Besides, from the sounds of it, she needs a tractor worse than she needs a husband."

Charley shrugged. "I doubt you'd stand a chance, anyway. I hear Max Daniel is planning to ask her out after Christmas—he's a rancher north of here. 'Course Tom Fox might beat him to the punch. A good-looking woman like Jenny can have her pick of the bachelors around here once folks decide we've given her enough time to settle in. Most folks think Christmas is time enough for a young woman like that to start dating again."

Zach grunted. Ever since he started making money at rodeoing, he'd had folks trying to get him to settle down. Made him nervous as a rope-tied calf every time a woman talked about it. Anyone with any sense could see that the life he'd led didn't prepare him for marriage.

Not that he didn't like women. He did. He just had sense enough to know his limitations. He didn't even have a year-round mailing address; he'd be a fool to think he would be any good at marriage.

"Yeah, well, it was only a thought," Charley said as he pointed to the back of the postal truck. "Now, you remember what I said about the camera back there. Edith promised Jenny pictures of her little boy with Santa, and I'll never hear the end of it if you don't remember to take one with him."

"Pictures." Zach grimaced. "I'm not much good at pictures."

"What? You can't tell me that. If you've ridden the rodeo circuit, you must be used to getting your picture taken," Charley said and then lowered his eyes. "That is, if you've ever won anything."

"I win," Zach said. He should tell the old man how many times he won.

"Well, then, you must have had your picture taken at least once."

Zach grunted. Once? Try a hundred times. "Well, the win photos—they're all right. But they're not, well, personal."

Zach didn't know how to explain his reluctance to have a picture of him in some family album along with pictures of babies and grandmas. He'd feel a fraud. A family photo album was one place he didn't belong.

"There's nothing to a Santa picture," Charley said, pushing ahead, anyway. "It's one of those cameras that prints out a picture while you wait. Jenny will even take the picture for you. And Edith said to leave the camera, in case Jenny wants to take other Christmas shots."

Zach nodded in defeat. He hoped Thunder would enjoy being taken care of by Charley here.

"And don't forget about old Mrs. Goussley. She has a sweet tooth. We always give her a few extra candy canes." Charley winked. "Say they're for her cats. She'll give them back if you say they're for her."

"Cats," Zach repeated bleakly.

"Mrs. Goussley likes her visit from Santa. She gets a kick out of the suit." Charley eyed Zach. "I know Delores got carried away this year with putting those flashing lights around Santa's belt, but you can keep them pressed off if you want. Plus the suit's warm—all that padding. Still, it might not be enough. Gets cold out there. Could drop to below zero before you get back."

"I've got a sheepskin coat if it does." Zach had put his duffel bag and the coat in the postal truck. The sheepskin was imitation, but of good enough quality to be worth a pretty penny. It wasn't something he'd leave behind. Not that he didn't trust the older man, but he'd worked enough rodeos to know never to leave his duffel with strangers.

"Oh, well then," Charley muttered as he stepped closer to the truck. "I'll just put this pie inside and let you get going. Remember, now, the brakes turn a little to the left if you happen to be going downhill."

Zach nodded. He was definitely going downhill. Playing Santa to an old lady and her cats. Zach "Lightning" Lucas. He shook his head and pulled his Stetson down farther.

He sure hoped no one who had the teeth to be eating something besides oatmeal saw him today. He didn't want to be recognized. People always wanted pictures of him. The real him. A snapshot of him dressed in a Santa suit might even make it onto a grocery store tabloid. He shuddered to think what the rodeo world would say if they saw him looking like this.

The reporter probably wouldn't even be kind enough to say Zach was doing it all for his sick horse. No, Zach would just be there looking like a fool for no good reason.

## Chapter Two

Jenny looked out the kitchen window again. Gray storm clouds almost covered the square butte west of their place. It was starting to snow, and the mail hadn't come yet. Mrs. Hargrove had told her that Charley might be late with the mail, but he'd see the package Jenny was expecting got to them. It wasn't much, but it had the few presents she had been able to get for the children, and she was anxious for them to arrive. Tomorrow was Christmas Eve day and, since it would be Sunday, there'd be no mail delivery then.

Mrs. Hargrove had driven out to see Jenny and the children the day after they'd arrived. She'd brought some homemade bread and jelly which had won over Andy's heart. She'd then won over Lisa because she had a bridal magazine for them all to look at. Mrs. Hargrove and Charley were getting married on the first Sunday of April and the older woman glowed when she spoke of it.

"You're all invited to the wedding, of course," Mrs. Hargrove had said. "We want to have lots of children around."

"You're sure?" Jenny had asked. "They can be distracting."

Mrs. Hargrove grinned. "I'm hoping they will be. Charley and I are simple folks. We don't need everyone staring at us."

That's when Mrs. Hargrove had won Jenny over. Since then, the older woman had become Jenny's closest friend. Just knowing that there were people like her in the small town of Dry Creek had convinced Jenny that God did want her and the children here.

Mrs. Hargrove had done some shopping for Jenny in Miles City. The box coming with the mail should have what she had ordered—a water pistol for Andy, a paint kit for Lisa and much-needed mittens and scarves for them both. Andy really wanted a cowboy outfit with a hat, and Lisa really wanted a princess tiara, but they were both too expensive and nowhere to be found in Miles City, anyway.

Maybe next year, Jenny consoled herself.

She'd surely think of a way to make some money soon. She had to. She'd just spent everything except a few hundred dollars filling the propane tank so the furnace would keep going for the next few months. If nothing else, she thought, I want to be generous with heat when it comes to our place.

*Our place.* She repeated the phrase to herself in satisfaction. Stephen had left them a wonderful place. This Christmas it would be enough that they had a home that was all their own, even if the roof leaked on the south side of the living room and the linoleum in the kitchen had more cracks than color left. Still, the place had three bedrooms and no landlord. They didn't have to worry about making too much noise or keeping the walls beige. Or paying the rent.

There was even a huge barn that would be useful if she got some goats. In the meantime, a cat from someplace had taken up residence in the barn, and the children had both started leaving food for it.

The barn was the final thing that convinced her that the move here would turn out all right. The agricultural guidebook Mrs. Hargrove had given her said this country was good for sheep, so Jenny supposed it would also be good for goats. She wasn't sure if she could make a living from raising goats, but she intended to find out. She'd already found a recipe in one of her farming magazines for goat cheese.

And, of course, she'd also need to look for a job after Christmas. She was hoping she might find something in Dry Creek since she'd have to go there every day, anyway, once she enrolled Lisa in the school in Miles City. The school bus stopped at the café to pick up the Dry Creek children and take them to the bigger town. Jenny had talked to the third-grade teacher, and they'd agreed Lisa could start in January. Surely by then Jenny would have the car running the way it should.

In the meantime, they were adjusting.

"Mom, I see her coming!" Andy's voice carried from the back bedroom. He was obviously looking out the window himself.

"Get down off those boxes, Andrew Joel." If he could see out the window, it meant he was standing on the boxes again. Jenny hadn't intended to leave everything in boxes for long. She just hadn't been able to buy dressers or bookshelves or cabinets—none of the furniture that stored things.

Jenny had sold all their furniture before leaving California. Stephen had said in his ramblings that there would be furniture in the house already.

He had been wrong, of course. Nothing had been as he described. She wouldn't have recognized the farm from his memories when she took her first look at the place that late afternoon several weeks ago. The day had been starting to grow dark and she had her headlights on when she drove over the hill to the property. Charley was following behind her.

Jenny doubted anything but thistle had grown on the place for the past ten years. The acreage was fenced, but half of the fence was down. The only trees were short scrub ones, and she'd already heard from someone before they left the store in Dry Creek that the creek Stephen remembered at the bottom of the coulee, the Big Dry Creek, had been dry for the past two years.

Still, this to be was their home. Charley had stayed that first day to help Jenny light the furnace. The electricity was off, but she had candles, and she told Charley they would be fine until she had a chance to sort things out the next day.

The older man had welcomed her again to Dry Creek and left. From that first day, things got better. It only took a few days for the children to figure out that they didn't need to stay inside the house. They had a freedom they had never known around Los Angeles.

If the children were content, Jenny could live without furniture for a few months. She'd told the kids they'd pretend they were camping. So far, they hadn't complained.

"But she's coming!" Andrew said as he ran out of the bedroom door and down the small hallway. "She's coming to get my letter."

"Oh, dear. I forgot." Jenny remembered that Mrs. Brown had promised Andy she'd take his letter special delivery to the North Pole so that Santa could read it before he began his trip tomorrow. Jenny had helped him write the letter, so she had known for days what it said. She just hadn't realized he wanted the letter mailed until recently. "I'm afraid it won't be Mrs. Brown getting the mail today. Charley is taking the route for her."

"Does he still have that runny pig?"

Charley had had a pig in the back of his pickup truck the last time he'd brought the mail.

"*Runt*. The pig was a runt. And, yes, I think he still has him."

"Can he find the North Pole?"

"I'm sure he can," Jenny said. Charley was

a nice man. She was sure he'd play along with Andy's fantasy. She'd wondered if Andy should still believe in Santa. If it weren't so soon after Stephen's death, she probably would have explained to him that Santa Claus wasn't real. After all, Andy would be five soon.

But it was all so complicated. Jenny worried that Andy never talked about Stephen's death. He was as close-mouthed as Lisa. Jenny had tried talking to them both, but they just didn't seem to have much to say.

Jenny knew Stephen had been a distant father, but surely the children felt something.

Stephen had made it plain to Jenny shortly after they married that he wasn't a family man. She wished he'd said so before they married. But he hadn't, and Jenny had hoped he would change—surely a man would care about his own children. But Stephen never had. Stephen had lived his life apart from the family as much as possible ever since their oldest, Lisa, was born.

No, it wouldn't hurt Andy to believe in Santa for another year.

Zach twisted the wheel to keep the postal truck on the road. Charley hadn't exaggerated when he'd complained about the ruts to the

Collins's place. No wonder the woman's car was down for the count. There probably wasn't a nut or bolt in the whole vehicle that hadn't been shaken to within an inch of its life.

The road matched the house at its end. A bright patch of white paint around the door made the rest of the house look even more faded. He suspected this Collins woman didn't know that paint needed to be applied in warmer, dryer weather. Of course, he supposed it did get the message across that someone was living there. Without that paint and the yellow curtains in the kitchen window, the place would look deserted.

The huge red barn a few hundred feet from the house looked as if it was in better shape than the house.

The land itself looked as though no one had ever cared for it. Flat and gray, it stretched out in all directions with nothing but half-melted lumps of old snowdrifts and a few scrub trees on it. The gray patches were gathering a coating of white as the snowflakes started to fall. In the distance Zach saw a few buttes rising up from the ground, but they were so far away he didn't pay them any attention.

A woman opened the door of the house as Zach pulled the postal truck to a stop. She was hugging an unbuttoned man's flannel shirt around her shoulders and was wearing a T-shirt and jeans. A young girl stood on one side of her and an even younger boy on the other.

Zach unlatched the side door and stepped out of the postal truck. The north wind was already turning bitter, so he walked along the south side of the truck until he reached the vehicle's back door. Cold, hard flakes of snow hit against his face.

Zach had given up and put the Santa beard and hat on before he even got to Mrs. Goussley's. It was the cookies that had done it. Every place he stopped, someone shoved a plate of homemade cookies into his hands. He explained that he wasn't Mrs. Brown—why, he wasn't even Charley—he wasn't entitled to any cookies. But no one listened. It was Christmas, they said, and he looked like a nice young man.

He hadn't been called a nice young man since he'd started riding rodeo. He was getting soft, he thought glumly as he yanked the furry red cap farther down on his head and snapped the fake white beard into place. The cardboard box marked "Collins" and the pie were all the mail left to deliver.

Zach lifted the two things up. It would only take a minute to get the box up to the porch.

Once there, he'd see about a quick Santa picture with the kids and head back to town. Maybe Thunder would be able to travel by then. If Zach was lucky, he'd be in the arms of that showgirl by Christmas after all.

Even from a distance Zach could see the woman was younger than he'd thought she would be. He'd guess her age at twenty-seven or twenty-eight. He shared Charley's surprise that she'd taken on a farm in the middle of Montana. He would expect someone like her to move into one of the cities like Billings or maybe Missoula. Someplace that had a video store and a beauty shop.

Not that it was any of his worry. She could live on the moon for all he cared.

"Package," Zach said when he got close enough to the porch to thrust the package at the woman. Short blond curls blew around her face, and up close he confirmed his opinion of her. Even in the cold, she would draw some attention in a crowd. The wind had turned her nose pink to match her cheeks.

Zach had a momentary wish he'd taken the Santa suit off before he'd made his last delivery. Lots of women had a weakness for cowboys. He'd never heard of a woman yet who thought a fat, polyester Santa was sexy.

Not that he was interested in what this woman or any woman in this part of Montana thought about him. What he'd told Charley had been true—he was just delivering the mail and then passing through.

If Zach had been paying attention to what he was doing instead of admiring the woman in front of him, he would have seen her eyes sooner. Startled blue eyes looked straight at him.

"It's the mail," Zach clarified. No one else had greeted him with anything remotely like panic. Maybe she thought he was some kind of kook. "The suit's for the old ladies. Well, that and the pictures. Mrs. Hargrove wanted you to have one with your kids."

"Where's Charley?"

"In some barn someplace looking after my horse."

"You've got a horse." The young boy looked around his mother's thigh and up at Zach. His eyes shone with wonder. "A real horse."

The two children stood on either side of the woman. The boy's jeans were neatly patched at the knees, and he obviously took his fair share of tumbles; the girl's clothes were well washed but showed no sign of stains or tears. Not even little ones. The boy's eyes had already welcomed Zach, but the girl's were more careful.

"He's as real as a horse can be, even when he's sick," Zach said. "In his day, he was the best bucking bronc around."

"Santa has reindeer—not horses," the young girl pointedly corrected Zach as she crossed her arms. Zach pegged her age at seven. Maybe eight. "You need to get the story straight."

"It's no story," Zach protested. "I'm not—"

The woman's eyes widened in even more alarm and Zach stopped. He looked back down at the young boy.

"—in a hurry," Zach fumbled. Were there still kids left that believed in Santa Claus? Apparently so. "I'm not in a hurry at all."

The woman smiled in relief.

Now, that woman should smile more often, Zach thought. She was pretty without the smile, but when she smiled she made him think of one of those soap ads where they try to picture springtime. It might be twenty degrees below zero on this porch right now, but when he looked at Mrs. Collins he could almost see the green meadow she should be walking through.

But, Zach reminded himself, he wasn't here to think of meadows. He was here to deliver the mail, snap a picture and give away the last of those bothersome candy canes.

"I have something for you in my pocket."

Zach had moved the last of the candy canes from the bag to his pocket several stops back. "Just let me set this box down inside the house and I'll get it out for you."

Zach didn't notice that the alarm on the woman's face turned to dismay.

"I can take the package," Jenny offered. She wasn't ready for company.

"No problem. I've got it," Zach said as he stepped up to the door the boy was opening.

"But I can—" Jenny started to repeat even as she watched the man walk into her kitchen. Great, she thought. Just what she needed— some man in a Santa suit seeing her house. Every man she had ever known expected a woman to keep a neat house. Stacks of boxes and fold-up furniture would hardly qualify as neat. She hoped the beard would hide his disapproval. Although, she told herself with a tilt of her chin, it wasn't any of his business what kind of a housekeeper she was.

## Chapter Three

"I haven't had a chance to get to town much yet," Jenny said defensively as she stepped through the kitchen doorway behind the man. She hadn't minded when Mrs. Hargrove had come inside and sat on one of the folding chairs, but a strange man was different. "I've been meaning to find some used furniture or something."

The man set the box and a foil-wrapped pie down on the kitchen counter and started patting his pockets.

The kitchen counter was covered with tiles so old the white had turned yellow, but Jenny had scrubbed the grout clean. The floor, too, was spotlessly clean even though the linoleum was cracked. No one could say the place was dirty, she reminded herself, even if they could say it lacked almost everything else to recommend it.

"I've asked about garage sales—then I'll be able to buy a few things," Jenny continued before realizing the man was not only not listening, but he hadn't even taken a good look around. He probably didn't realize that all that stood in the kitchen was a broom in one corner and the folding card table and chairs that sat square in the middle.

"I must have another candy cane here someplace." The Santa man turned and held up one candy cane. The plastic around the red-and-white cane was wrinkled and looked as if it had been slept on. "I'm sure I couldn't have given them all out already."

The man continued patting his pockets a little frantically. "I gave one for each of the cats—that was five—and a few extra when she said one of the cats was going to have kittens—and then she gave me that plate of cookies, and I had to give her some for that—but I should still have—"

Zach made another pass at checking the pocket on his right. The suit only had the two large pockets, and they had both been full of candy canes. He shouldn't have given so many to Mrs. Goussley and her cats. Not when two children were waiting at the end of the route. "Maybe one dropped out in the truck. I'll go see."

Zach smiled at the kids to show they could trust him. The boy smiled back, so excited he was almost spinning. The girl eyed Zach suspiciously. No smile there. She clearly had her doubts about him and the promised candy cane. Well, he didn't blame her. At least she wasn't whining about it.

Zach walked toward the door.

"I'll go with you," Jenny said, as she turned to the two children. "You two stay here."

"But, Mom, I gotta—"

"Stay here," the woman interrupted the young boy. "We'll be right back. I want to talk to Santa."

"But, Mom," the boy persisted. "I gotta—"

"Later. I need to talk to Santa alone." The young woman used her best mother voice. Gentle but firm. Zach forgot all about the candy canes. Maybe Santa did have a little sex appeal if an attractive young woman was willing to take a walk in freezing temperatures just to talk to him privately.

Of course, he knew that a woman like her was trouble. He'd feel hog-tied after the second date. He'd have to tell her he was just passing through. Zach took another look at the woman's face and hesitated. Maybe he was being too cautious about dating. Just because a second date was out of the question, that didn't mean a first date was impossible.

Even a woman like that wouldn't have expectations on a first date, would she? A first date was a test with no commitment whatsoever. And that's all it would be. One date. He could put off starting down to Vegas until morning and still make it. Maybe he should ask her out for dinner tonight. The one restaurant in Dry Creek looked a little casual for a big date, but people must go somewhere.

"Where do people go around here for fun?" Zach asked as he opened the door for the woman.

It was only four o'clock in the afternoon, but the cold pinched at Zach's nose and he was grateful for the warmth of that beard on his face. The temperature had dipped a few degrees just in the time they had been inside. A full-fledged storm was coming.

"Fun?" The woman looked at him blankly. She crossed her arms against the cold and walked out the door, headed toward the postal truck.

Zach closed the door and hurried to follow. He could see the goose bumps on her neck in the strip between her collar and her hair. Pinpricks of snow still swirled around in the wind. "You need to wear something heavier than that flannel shirt when you're outside."

The woman walked faster. Her teeth chattered so he could hardly make out her words. "It'll do."

Zach opened the passenger door to the postal truck. The handle was icy to his touch. "Here. Sit inside."

Zach closed the passenger door and quickly walked around to the driver's side.

"You've heard of the North Pole?" the woman asked when Zach was inside and seated.

"That some kind of night club?" Zach was feeling more hopeful. Now they were talking fun. Maybe he wouldn't even need to go to Vegas to find some Christmas cheer. The North Pole must be a place in Billings.

"Huh?" the woman looked bewildered.

"Charley there could watch the kids." Zach thought out loud. He felt a little bad about the kids, but Charley would treat them fine. He probably even had more of those candy canes. The kids could do without their mother for one night. Some kids would actually be glad to spend a night apart from their mother.

"The North Pole," the woman repeated as

if she had doubts about his mental abilities. "You know—that place where Santa Claus makes his toys."

"Oh." So much for night clubs. Zach reached up and turned on the heat. The engine was still warm and gave off a soft wave of hot air. "I didn't know you meant *that* North Pole. Sure, I know it."

"Well, Andy is going to give you a letter to deliver to Santa Claus at the North Pole. Just go along with it, okay?"

"Sure," Zach shrugged. "I'll tell him I ride my horse, Thunder, right up there every night."

Jenny frowned. "Don't overdo it. He's four, but he's not gullible."

Zach refrained from pointing out that the boy still believed in Santa Claus. "Anything you say."

Zach smiled.

Jenny frowned.

Zach got a glimpse of himself in the rearview mirror and frowned, too. No wonder the woman was still cool to him. He looked like a lunatic. His beard was crooked and looked as if it was made of yarn that some cat had chewed. Zach pulled the beard down past his chin and let it settle around his neck. He pushed the Santa hat far enough back on his head so that she could see his hair. That should make her relax.

It didn't. Jenny's frown turned to an expression of alarm. "You look just like that...that cowboy on the cereal box."

Zach relaxed. He was home free. She'd seen the Ranger boxes. "He's me—I mean, I'm him."

"But you can't be." Jenny tried not to stare at the man's face. His cheekbones were high; his eyebrows black and fierce looking when he wasn't smiling. It was the middle of winter and his tan was only partially faded. The golden flecks in his brown eyes saved his face from being too severe. Nothing saved it from being the handsomest face she had ever seen.

Jenny had dreamed of that face ever since Andy had convinced her to buy the first box of that cereal a year ago. She must have bought three dozen boxes this last year alone. And that wasn't the worst of it. She'd been talking to the box.

Jenny was a private person and she didn't admit her unhappiness to anyone. But, one morning at a solitary breakfast, she'd poured out her troubles to the face on the back of the box and she'd been talking to it ever since. Only the face on the box knew about her disappointment with her marriage. To the rest of the world, her marriage was fine and her husband was the good-natured man he appeared to be to others. But the box knew the truth.

She'd told that box things she wouldn't have admitted to a minister, and now it sat before her. She felt betrayed. Pictures on cereal boxes were not supposed to spring to life in front of your eyes.

"You just can't be him."

"Well, everybody's got to be somebody."

Jenny panicked. Not only was the face here, it was—unless she missed her guess—also teasing her. Maybe even flirting with her. It was awful. "You'll have to go."

Okay, Zach thought to himself. Definitely not a night clubber. Which was fine. He had his good time waiting in Vegas. "Just give me a minute to find another one of those candy canes and I'll be happy to head out. I need to get back before the storm hits, anyway."

Jenny looked up. "I thought you said you'd take a picture with Andy."

"I did, but I thought you were, well, in a hurry for me to leave."

"No, I'm just, well, I don't want to take more of your time. But a picture only takes a second."

Jenny forced herself to look the man in the face. It wasn't his fault she'd started talking to his picture. She had a moment's wild suspicion that Elmer, the old man who thought he could tell what every woman wanted, had sent this man out here to finally prove his point. But that was silly. No one could possibly know about her and this man's face. Could they?

Zach was talking. "Okay. Fine. I'm happy to take a picture. Whatever you want."

Jenny forced herself to smile. "It's just that you're the only Santa around."

Zach grunted. "No problem."

"And I appreciate you bringing out everything for Mrs. Hargrove. And the candy canes, too. That was very nice of you."

"The mail carrier bought the canes. Delores Brown. I'm just passing them out for her."

"Still…"

Zach noted that the woman's face had relaxed. The goose bumps had left. The air inside the truck wasn't white with trails of exhaled air. "Not a problem. I'll even tell that boy of yours I'll take his letter to Santa."

Jenny frowned. "You're not related to Elmer, are you?"

"Huh?"

"Never mind. I'm sorry I can't—I mean, I

don't date, anyway—not that you were asking me out." Jenny stopped in embarrassment.

"Oh, but I *was* asking you out. At least I was heading in that general direction."

Jenny couldn't help but notice he sounded a little too cheerful for someone who had just been turned down. "Well, I appreciate that. I'm just sorry I can't accept."

"It's okay," Zach felt around the side of his seat and found not one but two candy canes. Hallelujah! He'd soon be out of here. "I suppose you tried the cereal and didn't like it—or you thought the manufacturer shouldn't say it is the cereal real cowboys eat when everybody knows cowboys don't eat anything but beans and trail dust."

"No, actually, I like the cereal. And I think cowboys would like it if they had a chance to try it. It's great—real nutty."

Zach nodded and didn't make the obvious comparison. "So you like the cereal. You just object to the box."

Jenny nodded sheepishly. "I guess it is kind of odd."

"No problem." Zach smiled to show it was okay. He'd been bucked by broncs. He'd learned how to take his lumps in life. If the woman was that set against him, he'd let it be.

Better times were waiting for him. "I'll just take this other candy cane into the house and pick up the letter from—what's the kid's name again?"

"Andy."

"So I'll pick up the letter from Andy, do our bit with the camera and be on my way back to Dry Creek."

"Thank you for understanding."

Zach shrugged as he opened the driver's door on the postal truck. "Don't mention it."

To show there were no hard feelings, Zach walked around and opened the passenger door, as well. "Some folks think the picture on the box is just some dress-up modeling job. But it isn't. The cereal company asked to put my picture on the box because I won the All-Pro Championship in bronc riding five years in a row."

"Oh, I didn't think they used your picture because of your looks." Jenny gracefully stepped out of the truck and almost immediately folded her arms in front of her for warmth.

Zach admitted complete defeat. Most women found him attractive. He wasn't fool enough to go after one who didn't. Especially not when he was out in the middle of nowhere and the sky was turning a serious gray.

"Storm's coming," Zach offered as they walked toward the house. He suddenly understood why everyone in Dry Creek worried so much over this little family. He felt some of that same worry tugging at him. There wasn't another house around for miles. "You got enough supplies stored up and everything? A winter storm in southern Montana can be a fierce thing."

"I know that."

Zach wondered how she could know that. He didn't ask, but she must have caught the drift of his disbelieving thoughts.

"I may not have lived through one of the storms here, but I have a guidebook about Montana. It's got lots of information." Jenny told herself she had learned from her lack of an umbrella. She'd read the guidebook cover to cover. She was prepared now.

Zach groaned inside. The woman had learned about Montana storms from a guidebook. The few snowflakes that were falling had a dry sting to them. Zach knew that meant the coming storm would be cold enough to freeze a person. Some folks thought the large wet flakes signaled the worst storms, but they didn't. The wet flakes generally meant more snow, but the dry ones foretold a swift and merciless drop in temperature. And with the wind that could be dangerous.

"The electrical will probably go out. Are you set for that?"

Jenny turned to look at him squarely and lifted her chin. She was standing on her porch and she could still feel the pinch of the cold in her nose. She could see the sky was going deep gray and she could hear the grumbling in the air. "We have a propane furnace. And I have some oil lamps if the lights go out."

Zach grunted.

The door on the house popped open when they stepped near it. The little boy had been waiting for them to come back and must have heard their steps on the porch.

"Hi, there, Andy." Zach stepped inside behind Jenny. At least the boy liked him. Zach revised that opinion. Andy was looking at him as if he'd sprouted a second head.

"Santa Claus?"

Zach grabbed for his chin. He'd forgotten the beard.

Jenny met his eyes in alarm. She took a quick breath. "Santa shaved."

Zach slipped the beard back over his chin. But it was too late. The kid was bewildered. Then the confusion on Andy's face slowly cleared as though he finally understood a big secret. Zach felt a momentary pang, but then decided it was just as well the kid learned the truth about Santa Claus.

Zach looked over at Jenny. She was signaling him desperately to do something. Zach figured there wasn't much to be done.

"He'd find out someday, anyway—now that he's a big boy." Zach threw the boy a bone. He knelt down until his eyes were level with the boy's. "Isn't that right? You're a big boy and big boys can handle the truth about Santa Claus, can't you?"

Andy nodded happily.

Zach threw Jenny a self-righteous look. He might not be a parent, but he did know some things about little boys. "You're a real smart big boy to figure out Santa's secret." Zach noticed the girl who stood beside her mother. She rolled her eyes as if Zach was hopeless.

Andy nodded eagerly and leaned forward to whisper. "I know the secret. Santa's a cowboy—he's you—Lightnin' Lucas."

"Well, now, that's not exactly true." Zach stalled. Maybe he didn't understand a little boy's mind as much as he thought he did. "I am Zach Lightning Lucas—that's true—but I'm just wearing a Santa suit. I'm a pretend Santa."

"I have cowboy pajamas." Andy nodded happily as he danced from one foot to the other. "That's pretend. Want to see?"

"Sure, I guess." Zach looked up at Jenny to get direction.

Jenny gave a reluctant nod. The pajamas had been Andy's present last Christmas, and they were still his most prized possession. "Why don't you bring them out here and let Mr. Lucas see them when you give him your letter? I think he'll still take it for you."

Jenny lifted a questioning eyebrow at Zach.

Zach bristled. He was a man of his word. "Of course I'll still take the letter. I'll see the letter gets to the North Pole tonight. Before Santa leaves on his trip tomorrow. I'll take it personally."

"Can you fly?" Andy looked at him in awe. "Like the reindeer?"

Zach swallowed and shifted his weight onto his knee. "No, but I know the way to the North Pole and I can drive fast in my truck. Zoom. Zoom. Of course," he said, fumbling, "nobody should drive too fast."

Zach hoped the kid forgot this conversation before he turned sixteen and got his driving permit.

"Will you take me with you?"

Zach looked over at the little boy looking at

him with such shining trust. Like a shy deer, the boy had edged closer and closer to Zach as he knelt beside him until now the boy was practically leaning against Zach's shoulder. Zach had to swallow again. "Not this time."

"Why not? I'll be good."

Jenny looked down at the man and her boy and felt sad. Andy never said anything, but he clearly yearned for a father even more than he yearned to be a cowboy. Maybe after Christmas she should accept a date from Max Daniel, that single rancher up north who Mrs. Hargrove had mentioned might be interested in her. Max attended the Dry Creek church and Jenny had spoken with him briefly on the three Sundays she and the children had gone there. Even if Jenny didn't find him very exciting, he was stable.

Jenny knew she didn't want to marry, but she had the children to think about.

Besides, a date didn't mean she was making a commitment. And it would make her feel as though she was at least open to God's leading in that area. And who knew? Maybe she would go on a date with the man and feel something that might eventually lead to being willing to get married again. The whole thought depressed her.

"Of course you'll be good," Zach was saying

to Andy. "But you see, well, you have to stay and help your mother. There's a storm coming and she'll need a big boy like you to help her."

"Lisa's bigger. She can help."

Jenny looked at the helpless expression on Zach's face and almost laughed. Just watching him lifted her spirits. Not many men were a match for a determined four-year-old.

"Of course she can." Zach searched the room for the girl and didn't see her. He wondered where she had gone. "It's just that—" Zach had an inspiration "—Santa's too busy to see people before he takes his trip. He only talks to the elves."

The boy looked up in sudden worry. "But my letter."

"Oh, I'm sure he has time for letters." Zach started to sweat. He decided he was better off facing a bucking bronc like Black Demon than a child like the one in front of him. He understood a thousand pounds of angry horse better than he did this little boy.

"I'm sure Santa reads all his mail." Jenny took pity on them both. Andy had labored for a full afternoon on his Santa letter, patiently copying the letters Jenny had printed for him.

Jenny hoped that Mr. Lucas understood how precious the letter was he'd offered to deliver.

Andy hadn't thought of anything for days since he wrote that letter.

"Lisa can come, too." The little boy leaned closer to Zach and confided, "She told me there's no Santa at the North Pole." The boy's voice dropped to a whisper. "She has to do dishes for a month all by herself if I show her that Santa lives there. It's a bet."

Jenny saw her son's blond head leaning close to the man's dark one. The man's arm had gone around her son's shoulders and they were whispering about something she couldn't make out. She knew children liked their secrets, but she wasn't sure she wanted this cowboy to share them.

"Mr. Lucas needs to leave soon, Andy," Jenny reminded her son as she picked up the camera from the counter. Lisa had insisted she was too old for a Santa picture, so Jenny only had to worry about Andy. "Why don't you go get your letter for him, and I'll take your picture while you give it to him."

"It's here," Andy said as he moved away from Zach enough to pull a crumpled letter out of his pocket. He handed it up to Zach. "I've been saving it."

The camera flash went off as Jenny snapped a picture.

"I'll deliver it express mail." Zach blinked as he took the letter in his hand. The woman hadn't even given him time to force a smile. "You can trust the U.S. Postal Service." Zach saluted the boy even though, as far as he knew, the postal service had never had a salute of any kind. But it seemed to reassure the boy.

Zach stood up and looked at the woman. "If you want, you can try a second picture."

Jenny looked at him.

"I wasn't smiling." Zach almost swore. It wasn't his idea to have his picture in some family album, but if his picture was going to be there it seemed only right that he be smiling.

Jenny shrugged. "The beard covers most of your face, anyway."

Zach nodded. If the woman didn't care if Santa was smiling, he shouldn't care. It did make him wonder what Christmas was coming to, however. If anyone should be smiling at Christmas, it was Santa and his helpers. "It's your picture."

"Did you get my letter in the picture?" the boy asked.

The woman nodded.

"I drew the stamp myself." The boy looked up at Zach. "Mom said it was all right."

Zach bent down and shook the boy's hand

for further assurance. "It's just the right kind of stamp."

The kitchen had a window by the sink and one on the opposite wall. The sky was gray out of both windows, and Zach heard the rattle of the wind as it gathered force.

He watched as Jenny pulled the stub of a picture out of the camera.

"Here." Jenny held the camera out to him.

Zach shook his head. "Charley said you were to keep it over the holidays in case you want to take more pictures."

"Well, that's kind of you."

"Not me. It belongs to Mrs. Hargrove." Zach shuffled his feet. He wasn't used to getting so much credit for things he didn't even do.

"I better get out of here before the storm hits." Zach pulled his Santa hat back on his head. No one had flipped any light switches, and the light coming into the windows was thin. Fortunately, he could hear the hum of the furnace and a floor vent blew a steady stream of warm air into the room. At least the family had heat.

Zach looked over at the woman who held a still-developing picture in her hand. "You're sure you'll be all right now in this storm? If you need to call anyone on the phone to come sit this storm out with you, I'd do it now. The lines might go down anytime now."

"Thanks. I'll do that," Jenny said. She smiled confidently as if she had someone to call.

Zach nodded. He figured that the cereal box wasn't the only reason the woman wouldn't go out with him. She must have a boyfriend. Well, he shouldn't be surprised. Charley had as much as told him she did. Some rancher—what was his name? Max something.

"Well, I'll leave, then," Zach said as he walked toward the door. "I'll close the door quick behind me so you keep your heat in."

Jenny watched the man walk to the door. Suddenly she didn't want him to leave. There was a blizzard coming and she didn't know what to expect. Even a cereal-box cowboy was better than no one when it came to facing a storm. But she couldn't ask him to stay. He was a stranger, for goodness sake. Just because she was used to telling her troubles to his face didn't mean he had any obligation to her.

"You've got holiday plans?" she squeaked out as he put his hand on the doorknob.

He turned around and looked at her. "Vegas."

"Oh. I see. Well, have fun."

Jenny could kick herself. Of course, the

man had plans. It was Christmas, after all. Everyone had plans.

"Thanks." Zach hesitated. "I could change them if—"

"Of course you can't change them." Jenny stiffened her resolve. "I was just asking because I…I mean we…we have plans of our own and I was hoping you had plans, too."

"I see. Thanks." Zach turned the knob this time. No sense staying where someone had plans that didn't include him.

Zach leaned into the wind as he walked to the postal truck. The sky was getting darker in the east. A spray of snowflakes hit his face, even with the beard pulled up. He noticed that he hadn't closed the back door to the postal truck completely. He walked over and snapped it shut. He didn't want a chill at his back while he raced this storm back to Dry Creek.

Zach started the engine on the postal truck and released the brake. Time to get back. It was probably too late to beat the storm to the pass. Unless he missed his guess, he'd be sleeping in the horse trailer tonight while Thunder boarded at Charley's barn. In a few hours no one would be doing much driving. Zach just hoped he made it back to Dry Creek before the roads were snowed shut.

He could feel the hard boards of that trailer on his back already. It was going to be some merry Christmas.

## Chapter Four

Andy wanted a peanut butter sandwich.

"Just let me be sure the oil lamp is filled and I'll make you one," Jenny said as she watched the taillights of the postal truck pull away. The red lights were the only bright thing in the dark gray of the afternoon. A layer of snow had already fallen and she could see the tire tracks of the truck.

Jenny had made a mental list over a week ago of the things she needed to do to prepare for a winter storm. Making sure the lamp was full was the first one. The other was to be sure the curtains were drawn on all the windows so that there was a little extra insulation. Mrs. Hargrove had insisted Jenny buy a case of tuna and another of assorted soup when she moved here. The older woman had also urged her to always keep the propane tank that fed the furnace at least half-full.

"Heat and food is all you really need," the older woman had said. "If your pipes freeze you'll more than likely still have snow around that you can melt for water. Not that it's as pure as you might think. I'd get some water filters if I were you and run the melted water through them. Outside of that, keep healthy and you'll do fine."

Jenny didn't feel as if she was doing fine. She hadn't been able to get any filters for water. But the small stove in the kitchen fed off the propane tank out back so she could use that to boil the water if necessary.

Just keep focused, she reminded herself. Like Mrs. Hargrove had said, she'd do just fine. Ten minutes passed before she realized Mrs. Hargrove was wrong. Jenny wasn't fine. She'd made one big mistake. The number one rule of surviving a blizzard with your children was to actually have your children inside the house with you. Andy was here, but Lisa was gone.

Jenny searched every room in the house twice before Andy confessed that Lisa had sneaked out the door in the laundry room and hid in the back of the postal truck. Jenny was accustomed to watching Andy. He was the one who got into trouble and scrapes. She never had to worry about Lisa.

"We got a bet going," Andy explained without a trace of worry. "Lisa's gonna go see all about Santa and let me know."

Jenny's heart stopped. "You mean she went off alone!"

"The Lightning man's with her," Andy said calmly. "He'll take care of her until they get to Santa's."

"But Mr. Lucas is going to Las Vegas!"

"Not until he takes my letter to the North Pole. He promised."

Jenny was speechless. Her daughter had run off with some cowboy on his way to Vegas, and she was only eight years old.

"He'll bring her right back," Jenny promised herself aloud. *Dear Lord. The man has to bring her back.* "When he sees her in the truck, he'll bring her right back."

But what if he didn't see her? Lisa was obviously hidden or she'd be back already. Unless the man was—Jenny stopped herself. No, she wouldn't even think that. She was sure he wasn't that kind of a person. After all, she knew he hadn't deliberately taken Lisa.

Jenny looked out the window. The tracks left

by the postal truck had been filled in with new snow.

He's not going to see Lisa in time to bring her back, Jenny thought to herself in despair. Oh, she supposed he would leave her with Charley—when Jenny thought about it she wasn't completely worried that the man would actually want to take Lisa to Las Vegas with him—but still, Lisa would miss Christmas. Lisa had never been away from home at Christmas before.

Jenny looked around. She wished now that she had swallowed her pride and asked someone to bring them a Christmas tree from Miles City. She had told herself it would be okay for this Christmas to be plain. Her children would understand and share her grate-fulness that they had a new home. They'd hang their stockings and read the Christmas story and that would be enough.

But she was wrong. Lisa wouldn't have come up with a ridiculous bet like this for Andy if they had both been busy decorating a tree or putting gumdrops on cookies. Her children needed Christmas and she had failed to give it to them. It wasn't even grief that had stopped her from doing what she should. She had just been so intent on proving that they belonged here on this farm that she'd forgotten how important Christmas was.

Zach swore under his breath. The snow blew thicker every minute. Enough of it covered the road so that he couldn't make out the ruts. He was lucky to keep this tin can of a postal truck on the dirt road. But the snow wasn't his big problem. His big problem sat on the passenger seat next to him.

"I knew you couldn't go to the North Pole," the girl said smugly as she bit into another oatmeal cookie. "There is no North Pole."

Zach gritted his teeth. "Didn't your mom teach you not to go off with strangers?"

He'd been halfway back to Dry Creek when he'd heard the muffled sneeze from the back of the postal truck and had been so startled he'd almost driven off the road. In fact, he did pull to the side of the road so he could twist around and take a good look back there. The girl had been hiding under his sheepskin coat.

"We're not in Los Angeles anymore." The girl took another bite of cookie. "There aren't any strangers here. Only farmers."

Zach had given her the plate of cookies he had gotten from Mrs. Goussley. So far she'd managed to polish off half of them.

"There are things to be careful about in Montana, too."

"I know." The girl brushed the crumbs off her jacket sleeve. "My mom read about them in that book. There's snakes in the coulee. And bees in the summer."

"And strangers. Weird people are everywhere. You can never be too careful with strangers."

The girl shrugged. "You got any milk?"

"Of course not, this is a postal truck not a lunch truck."

Zach strained to see through the snowstorm outside his windshield. He'd guess there was four inches of snow so far on the ground— maybe more. He hoped that was the final turn to the Collins place up ahead.

"Your mother's going to be worried. She won't know where you are."

"Andy will tell her. He can't keep a secret."

Zach hoped the girl's mother didn't jump to any wild ideas like that maybe he had asked the girl to come with him. He had given her the candy cane, but no mother would think that would be enough to entice a child to climb into his truck. Of course, Zach slowly realized, he had said he was going to see Santa. A court of law might see that as enticement enough for any child.

Zach started to sweat. He'd best get this little one home soon. "Ah, good, that *is* the turn."

The snow was blowing so much he could only make out the outline of the house and the yellow glow of the windows.

Jenny thought she heard the sounds of a car and ran to the window. An hour had passed since Mr. Lucas had left, and the day had turned to evening. Jenny opened the door to see better. Stinging snow hit her face, but she only leaned out farther to try to see more clearly. If it weren't for those red and green lights on the postal truck, Jenny wouldn't have been sure it was Mr. Lucas coming back up her long driveway.

The truck stopped a few feet from the porch, and the lights went out. The driver's door opened and Jenny breathed easier. It was him.

"Lisa!" The wind blew the call away from Jenny and she wasn't sure her daughter would hear it, but the man did and he gave her a reassuring wave as he walked around to the passenger side of the truck.

Her daughter started to walk to the porch, but the wind made her stumble. The man picked her up and took her up the steps in long strides. Snow clung to her daughter's hair as the cowboy brought her across the porch and into the door that Jenny held open.

The temperature had dropped even more than Zach had figured when he was inside the truck. He knew that was why the girl clung to his neck. All that Santa suit polyester was warm and fuzzy. Still, he liked having her nestled there. It made him feel, well, a little fatherly, he thought defensively. Nothing wrong with that.

"Lisa! Are you all right, honey?" The woman opened her arms, and Zach reluctantly gave the girl to her.

"She's fine," Zach said curtly.

"I don't feel so good," the girl moaned.

"What'd you do to her?" Jenny shifted Lisa in her arms and glared at Zach.

"Me?" Zach looked around. Even the boy was looking at him suspiciously. "All I did was give her the candy cane and some cookies."

"You did find Santa's!" Andy gave a triumphant war whoop and jumped down off the chair where he was sitting. "No more dishes."

"The cookies came from Mrs. Goussley. Honest, you can call her up on the phone and ask her."

"That won't be necessary." Jenny set Lisa down on the floor and knelt at her eye level. "How many cookies did you eat?"

Lisa gave Zach a look of appeal.

"They were oatmeal cookies," Zach offered in her defense. He hadn't even counted how many were on that plate. "Oatmeal is good for you. Builds bones or something."

Jenny reached over and smoothed down her daughter's hair. It had been a long time since Lisa had been disobedient. Or done anything like eat too many cookies. It was good to see her daughter be a child again. "I guess a few extra cookies won't hurt anything."

A gust of wind rattled the house, and the overhead light flickered.

"I hope you have that lamp handy." Zach looked out the kitchen window. The sky was completely dark now, but he could see flakes of snow being whipped past the glass by the wind. "I should call Charley, too, before everything goes down."

"The phone's over there." Jenny pointed to the wall opposite the sink.

"Did you get a chance to make your call earlier?" Zach stepped over to the phone. Whoever she had been planning to call hadn't been much help to her. If she had called Zach with a storm like this on the way, he'd have been on her doorstep by now.

"I, ah, I thought I'd wait."

Zach pulled a slip of paper out of his pocket.

Charley had written his phone number on the same page he'd written the other instructions. Zach dialed.

"This is Zach Lucas." The phone only rang once before it was answered; Charley must have been waiting for a call. "I'm at Jenny's—"

"I'm so glad someone's there! Edith just called. There's a real blizzard coming through and she's worried—"

Another gust of wind hit the house and the phone went dead. Then the overhead light in the kitchen flickered again before it went out. Jenny's heart stopped. Her house was completely dark. There was no moon outside to provide even a soft hint of light. There was nothing. Just the howl of the wind and the rattle of the windows. Followed by a whimper and the shuffle of little feet.

"Stay still, Andy, I'll come to you." Jenny said as she slid one foot out across the kitchen floor. Andy didn't like the dark. She had to get to him. He had nightmares.

"That's okay. I've got him," Zach said as he felt the boy's arms grab his thigh and hug tightly. Zach bent down to lift Andy up in his arms. "We're just fine, aren't we, partner? It's just a little darkness."

The boy burrowed into Zach's fuzzy suit.

There was something about a Santa suit, Zach thought to himself. Even a crazy Santa suit like the one Mrs. Hargrove had put together. It made the kids feel at home with him. He realized with surprise that he kind of liked it.

"I don't like the dark," Andy whispered softly.

"It's okay," Zach muttered as he shifted his arm so one of his hands would be free to feel the grooves along the belt of the Santa suit. If he remembered Charley's words correctly, there was a switch here someplace that would turn on the flashing lights surrounding the belt. Zach had only seen the lights flash for a minute or two when Charley first asked him to put on the suit.

Jenny kept taking small steps in the general direction of her son. What had made Andy slide over and grab on to the cowboy? She had been as close to Andy as the cowboy had been. "Mama's coming."

Zach's hand found the switch on the belt at the same time as he smelled the perfume. He stopped to take another breath. It was a simple perfume—peach, if he wasn't mistaken. But it made him want to keep the darkness around him for just a minute or two longer.

Jenny reached out to where she thought

Andy was and touched the cowboy's arm instead. The softness of the Santa suit could not hide the solid steel of the man's muscle. Jenny knew she should move her hand when she discovered it was the cowboy she was touching and not her son, but she didn't. It was dark all around her and he was an anchor.

"Jenny?"

Jenny snatched her hand away from his arm. She was glad it was dark enough to hide the fierce blush she was sure was on her face. "I'm just worried about Andy."

"Of course," Zach shifted the boy's weight in his arms. "He's right here."

Jenny was close enough to sense the cowboy turning his body slightly so that her son was in the arm closest to her. Jenny reached out her hand again. This time she felt Andy's soft hair. She also felt the edge of Zach's shoulder.

It was ten degrees below zero outside and only about fifty degrees above zero inside the house, but Zach felt as if he didn't need to see another fire again as long as he lived. Jenny's touch had been tentative, but it scorched him.

"Can you hold him while I get the lamp?" Jenny asked.

"You got oil in the lamp already?"

"It's right next to it." Jenny felt disoriented. The sink had to be in that direction. "Under the sink."

Zach groaned. "You better light me up, then, so you don't break your neck walking over there."

"What?"

"It's the belt," Zach interrupted. "It's got built-in Christmas lights. I had the switch a minute ago, but I had to let go when I moved Andy."

"But how do I…?"

"Just feel along the belt until you come to a clicker kind of a thing. It attaches to the batteries."

"Your belt?"

Zach's mouth went dry at the breathless way she said it—as if he were asking her to do something a whole lot more intimate than turn on some lights. "It's about where Andy's feet are."

Jenny moved her hands away from Andy's hair and let them slide down Andy's back until the man shifted her son in his arms and suddenly her hands were sliding down the man's torso. Even the softness of the Santa suit couldn't hide the lean muscles of his chest and then his stomach underneath.

"I can't find it." Jenny stopped. It suddenly occurred to her she didn't want to go too low.

But she left her hand on his stomach. The whole world was dark around her and she wanted an anchor. Besides, she could hear his breathing.

Zach felt his breath catch. He shifted slightly to balance Andy in his left arm. He put his right hand over the one that Jenny had on his stomach. It wasn't until he touched her that he felt her pulse. Her heart was fluttering like a bird's.

"Scared?" Zach whispered.

"Me?" Jenny braced herself. It was only a man's stomach for goodness sake. "No, I'm fine."

"Good. I'd begun to worry I scared you with what I said about storms earlier. There's nothing to worry about. We'll be fine."

Jenny had completely forgotten about the storm. "Of course."

Zach reluctantly guided Jenny's hand to his belt buckle. He realized he could have just flipped the switch on his belt himself, but it was much more satisfying to feel Jenny's hand under his.

"I found it." Jenny felt the ridge of a button on the side of the smooth plastic of the belt. She slid the button to the right.

"That's it!"

A dozen tiny lights flickered. The kitchen was no longer dark. Instead, long shadows filled the corners and a soft glow surrounded Santa.

"Mama." Lisa ran to Jenny and stood beside her.

Zach felt as if time had stopped. There was just enough light in the kitchen to see Jenny's eyes. Zach didn't even realize he was staring at her eyes until she blinked.

"I better go get the lamp." Jenny didn't move. She meant to move, but she didn't. In the light coming from Zach's belt, the man looked more like his cereal picture than he had since he'd pulled down his beard. It was his eyes, Jenny thought to herself. He was looking at her as if she'd just given him a championship trophy.

"I didn't know those lights would work so well." Zach tried to rein his mind back to the present. He would start counting to ten if he had to—he couldn't stand there staring at the woman. She'd think he was a lunatic.

"Oh." So that was it, Jenny thought. That's what pleased him so much. Men and their mechanical toys. "Yeah, they're something. Great lights."

Zach felt Andy squirm in his arms.

"I'm hungry," Andy said as he wiggled his way down Zach until he reached the floor.

"Let me get the lamp set up first." Jenny patted

Andy on the head as she turned toward the counter. "Then I'll see what we can fix for dinner."

Jenny mentally catalogued the cans in her cupboard. She wished Mrs. Hargrove had warned her to keep more than soup on hand for blizzards. She didn't have anything suitable for company. "I'm afraid it won't be fancy."

"I don't need fancy," Zach said.

"Mama, what about—" Lisa said suddenly as she lifted worried eyes to her mother. "I mean, I know she's a wild cat, but—?

"You have a cat?" Zach asked. This family barely looked as though they could take care of themselves. What were they doing with a pet?

"She's not ours, but she lives in our barn," Jenny said. "We feed her and—well, I'll put together a dish of something."

"I'll take it out," Zach said. He couldn't bear the thought of Jenny going out in this kind of weather. "You could get lost on the way back."

"I wouldn't get lost. I already strung a rope out to the barn from here."

Zach grunted. At least the guidebook had one good tip in it.

"Maybe," Jenny hesitated and then pressed on. "Maybe you could build a fire in the wood stove when you're out there. It's in the side room with the bed. Charley brought us a load of wood one day and we put most of it out there. It's going to be cold tonight."

"You'll burn the place down doing that if no one's out there. Tell me you haven't been doing that."

"Well, no, but it hasn't been this cold yet. I'd say you should bring the cat into the house, but I don't think you could catch her."

"She's wild," Andy added solemnly.

Zach nodded. Of course, this little family couldn't have an easy pet if they had to have one. "I'll take a look when I'm out there."

Jenny opened a can of tuna and gave it to Zach for the cat.

"We'll have something hot to eat when you get back," Jenny said as Zach started for the door. "And the end of the rope is tied to the post by the porch. The guidebook—"

"I know," Zach said as he opened the door. "The guidebook said to tie it there."

One hour later they sat down to the table and there wasn't one hot thing on it. Even soup was impossible. "I never thought the pipes would be a problem. I should have kept the can of tuna for us."

The outside pipe on the propane stove had

shaken loose in the wind. Zach had capped it off when he came back from the barn, but he needed better light to fix it completely.

"This is just fine." Zach grinned. They were having cereal for dinner. His cereal. "I didn't know you ate this stuff."

"It's my favorite." Andy pushed his chair closer to Zach before he climbed up on it.

"I thought we should use up the milk up since the refrigerator is off." Jenny set a plate of bread on the table and sat down. "I had a coupon for the cereal."

"So you're just trying the cereal out?"

"I wouldn't say that exactly." Jenny casually turned the cereal box so the man's face wasn't staring at her. "We eat lots of kinds of cereal."

"It's my favorite," Andy repeated as he picked up his spoon and waved it around. "Cowboys eat it."

"It's only your favorite because Mom bought a ton of it." Lisa unfolded the napkin by her plate.

"Mr. Lucas doesn't want to hear about what we eat." Especially not how much of his cereal we eat, Jenny thought frantically. "Let's pray."

Zach looked around. Three heads bowed in unison. And then three sets of hands reached out to grab a hand. Zach was new to this prayer business, but he figured out he was supposed to link up with Andy and Lisa. That wasn't so bad.

"Lord, we thank You for the food You have provided," Jenny prayed. "Keep us all safe and warm—"

"The cat, too," Andy added.

"The cat, too," Jenny agreed. "Be with us in this blizzard of yours. We ask this in the name of our Savior, Jesus Christ. Amen."

Zach blinked when he looked up and opened his eyes. His rodeo friends wouldn't believe he'd just prayed. Well, maybe *he* hadn't prayed, but it was as close as he'd come in his life. It made him kind of nervous. He wondered if God had been listening.

Zach had nothing against God. He guessed he just didn't know anything about Him. Not that he was about to display his ignorance on the matter right here at the dinner table. He'd sometimes wondered what kind of people believed in God, though. Really believed. Now he knew.

Jenny noticed Zach was looking at her as though he wondered what he was doing here at the table with her and the children. She supposed this wasn't the kind of situation he was used to. Well, they'd just have to make the best of it.

"We should talk about—" She tried to remember what single people like Zach talked about. "We should talk about… That's it…" Jenny turned to face the man. "How was your day today?"

Zach watched Andy take a spoonful of the cereal dry. He could hear him crunching away. "My horse got sick, but I ended up having a good time delivering the mail. Met some nice people. How was your day?"

"Oh, your horse. Did Charley get a chance to say how he was before the phone line went dead?"

"I'm sure he's fine. Charley said earlier he thought it was just a low-grade fever." Zach noticed Jenny hadn't answered his question. Now what would a mother with small children do during the day? "And your day was no doubt spent getting ready for Christmas."

Jenny gasped and dropped her spoon on the table.

"What'd I say?" Even in the dark of the kitchen, Zach could tell he'd asked the wrong question.

"Nothing. It's just—" Jenny looked at her two children sitting one on each side of the stranger who should be a stranger but who wasn't because his eyes were looking straight at her just the way he did from the cereal box. She couldn't keep it in any longer. She was used to making her confessions to that face. "I'm a terrible mother."

Zach saw the tear in her eye before she bent her head down, and he said the only thing he could. "That can't be true."

Jenny looked up at him. "I don't have a proper Christmas for my children, and that's why Lisa ran away with you."

"Lisa didn't run away with me. She didn't even run away, really. She had a bet she wanted to win."

"Yeah, Mama. I wouldn't run away. I just wanted to show Andy that there's no Santa at the North Pole."

"See what I mean?" Jenny wailed.

Zach half nodded. He didn't see at all, but he could tell the woman needed sympathy. "It's a shame they make all this fuss about a day—all it is is December twenty-fifth. Just the day after December twenty-fourth. No need to go on so."

Zach heard three gasps all at the same time. One good thing—he was pretty sure Jenny's tears had stopped.

"But Christmas is the birthday of Jesus," Lisa announced primly. "The Savior of the whole world."

"All children need a Christmas," Jenny said at the same time.

"Don't you believe in Christmas?" Andy cut right to the important question. His eyes were wide in shock.

Zach squirmed and did the only manly thing he could. He lied. "Sure I believe in Christmas."

Jenny looked at him skeptically.

"Christmas just doesn't believe in me," Zach added softly.

"Well, surely you're going to celebrate Christmas," Jenny said. It was really none of her business, but everyone needed to celebrate something. And then she remembered that he was. "Of course, that's why you're going to Las Vegas."

Zach snorted. "I'm not going there to celebrate Christmas. I'm going there to forget there is such a miserable day."

"But I thought you had plans. That you were meeting a friend, or…" Jenny squinted at him. Surely nobody went to Las Vegas to be alone for the holidays. Come to think of it, it wasn't that easy to just go alone to Las Vegas at Christmas, especially without planning. "You won't get a hotel room, you know. Not over the holidays. All the hotels will be booked."

Hotel rooms all across the country were booked on holiday weekends. Everyone knew that.

"Patti already has a room for me."

"I see." Jenny's voice tightened.

Jenny didn't know why she cared that the person he was driving hundreds of miles to see was a woman. And not just any woman. A woman with a name. She should be glad he was driving off to meet some woman. It would keep her focused. The last thing she or her family needed was a man like him around. If they had a man in the family at all, they needed someone stable. Someone who would be a good husband and a father. Someone who didn't make her feel this way. "Well then, you don't have to worry about reservations."

Zach nodded.

Jenny knew she should let it go, but she didn't. "Maybe you'll see a show while you're there. I hear they have some wonderful Christmas shows. Ice skating, I suppose."

"You're thinking of the family shows. The kind of show Patti and the girls do isn't what you'd call family fare."

"This Patti—she's a singer?"

Zach shook his head. "Naw, she's just one of the showgirls."

"With the feathers in her hair?" Jenny knew what those showgirls wore and didn't wear. "She must be very pretty."

"I suppose so."

Jenny stiffened. "Of course she's pretty. They all are."

Zach told himself Patti would have to be pretty. He'd only spent several hours with her last year. He knew she was a blonde. But outside of that… "I don't remember her eyes."

"Well, maybe you should try looking at her eyes instead of—" Jenny broke off. Her children were at the table. Besides, it was none of her business who or what the cowboy admired. "Would you like some more cereal?"

"You know that showgirl stuff is mostly aerobics." Zach took the cereal box that Jenny offered.

"Aerobics?"

"Like cheerleading," Zach said firmly as he poured more cereal into his bowl. "Yeah, it's like cheerleading. Only with feathers in the hair and a swimsuit full of sequins."

"Mama was a cheerleader," Lisa offered proudly as she paused with her spoon halfway to her mouth. "Weren't you, Mama?"

"A long time ago."

"Really?"

"A very long time ago."

"We still have her pom-poms," Lisa said as she set down her spoon. "She didn't have any feathers or a swimming suit. She was a great cheerleader, though."

"I'm sure she was." Zach had a vision of Jenny bouncing around doing cheers. He wasn't sure it was at all the sort of vision he should have while he sat at the table with her children eating cereal. "She must have been wonderful—even without the feathers."

Jenny could feel the blush on her cheeks. She needed to change the subject. "I don't know why I kept those pom-poms. I didn't even pack an umbrella and I had those silly things along."

"Memories," Zach said.

"I guess." Jenny remembered she'd been happy in high school. Sometimes just looking at the pom-poms made her smile.

Everyone was silent for a bit.

"The snow should be gone by tomorrow," Jenny finally said. "It's too early to have a blizzard that sticks. You should still be able to make it out of here and catch your show."

Zach looked at her as if she was crazy. "What makes you think that?"

"The guidebook says—"

Zach snorted. "You have that guidebook here? Let me see it. I can practically guarantee you that this blizzard will last forty-eight hours."

"But that's impossible." Jenny looked stunned. She had come to rely on that guide-book. "Montana doesn't have long blizzards before Christmas."

"Tell that to the sky," Zach said.

Jenny would tell it to the sky if she thought there was any hope the sky would listen. "So you'll be here for Christmas."

"Looks like it."

"I'm afraid it won't be nearly as exciting as Las Vegas," Jenny said. Surely he would be able to leave tomorrow. The postal truck was a four-wheel-drive. It could go places her car couldn't go even when it was running. The house suddenly felt much too small, and the Christmas she'd planned much too humble to share with this man. "We don't even have a tree."

Zach felt the collar of his shirt get smaller and he swallowed. "I'm not worried about a tree. They aren't anything but a fire hazard, anyway."

"You don't like Christmas trees?" Lisa asked him in a voice that suggested he hated babies.

"Well, I…I don't have anything against them, I guess." Zach tried to make amends. "Especially if they don't have lights on them."

"No lights!" Lisa scoffed at him. "If there's no lights, it's not even a Christmas tree. Everyone knows that."

Jenny knew she should have tried harder to get a tree. Christmas was important to children. Well, it wasn't too late. "I'm going to go out tomorrow and get us a Christmas tree."

"Really?" Lisa turned to her mother breathlessly. "You are?"

"Of course," Jenny said. "This is Montana. There's lots of trees around. It might not be a pine tree like the ones we used to have in Los Angeles, but I can find something to decorate."

"It'll be twenty below zero tomorrow." Zach thought he should mention the fact. "You'll freeze to death."

"Tomorrow will be a fine day." Jenny lifted her chin. "Montana blizzards this time of year never last."

Zach groaned. Even if the sun did shine tomorrow, he couldn't leave this family in this kind of weather. They'd never make it through Christmas without help, the way they were carrying on. Jenny would freeze out there trying to chop down some fool sage bush. "And don't try baking any Christmas cookies until that propane line is fixed."

"Cookies," Andy sighed blissfully as he looked at Zach. "Are you going to make us some Christmas cookies?"

"Me?" Zach didn't like the trusting look in the boy's eyes. "I don't cook."

"I'll help you," Andy said, his trust not wavering. "I know how to stir. We can make cookies, can't we, Mom?"

Jenny looked at her son. She'd never seen him this anxious to spend time with a man before. It must be because Zach was a cowboy. How could she explain to her son that this man was not the kind of man to put on an apron and bake cookies with a little boy. "Mr. Lucas might be busy."

Fortunately, Andy didn't ask what the man would be busy doing. "Busy" was the excuse his father had always used when Andy asked to do anything with him.

Zach watched the joy flow out of Andy's eyes, and he found he didn't like it. "I guess I could learn to make cookies. How hard can it be?"

"Really?" Andy's eyes shone again.

"What?" Jenny stared at Zach as if he'd offered to fly to the stars. "Are you sure?"

Zach nodded. He wasn't going soft, he told

himself. He was snowed in with this family. Snowbound, really. He was just making the best of a bad situation. Anyone would do the same. It was that time of year, after all.

He sure hoped he wasn't going soft.

## Chapter Five

Jenny had no choice but to follow the cereal cowboy and her son deeper into the house. They'd all cleared their bowls off the card table, and there was nothing to keep them in the kitchen.

"We haven't been here a month yet." Jenny carried a flashlight even though Zach and his lit belt showed everyone the way. The living room was almost empty. She had a cork bulletin board hanging on one wall that was covered with snapshots of the kids, but it was the only thing hanging on the walls. A few boxes stood along the other wall. The flaps of the boxes were pulled up and showed a jumble of children's books. They didn't have a television set, so the children each picked a favorite story each night and they sat together while

Jenny read to them. Lisa loved fairy tales. Andy liked animal books.

"We're camping," Andy confided in a loud whisper as he led Zach through the living room. "That's why we don't need furniture."

Jenny winced. The one piece of furniture that had been there to welcome them was a rust-colored sofa that sagged and had a grease spot on the right cushion. Jenny had covered it with a light-blue afghan she had knit when she was pregnant with Andy. It was a baby's afghan, but she'd made it large and it almost covered the sofa. "I plan to get some used furniture just as soon as I can get to Billings."

"Yeah, I hear your car isn't working," Zach said as he followed Andy's lead and sat down on the sofa. "Charley said it was the radiator."

No sooner had Zach settled on the sofa than Andy burrowed into the cushion next to Zach's elbow and whispered, "Charley—he's got a pig."

"Is that right?" Zach looked down at the boy. The living room was full of crazy red and green shadows from the Christmas lights on the Santa belt, but no matter what shade of light surrounded the boy's face it just seemed to keep shining. Zach had a pang of wistfulness knowing he'd never been that trusting. Certainly not at four years old. Maybe not even at four months. Not with the kind of parents he'd had. He'd had to learn to take care of himself early. By the time he was Andy's age, he was taking care of his alcoholic parents as well as himself.

"I've got pigs, too," Andy said as he jumped off the sofa and headed toward the books. "They huffed and puffed."

Zach felt as if he'd fallen down a rabbit hole.

"It was the wolf that huffed and puffed," Jenny clarified. She had to admit that the cowboy was taking her sparse furnishings better than she would have expected. He didn't look around with anything like pity in his brown eyes.

Andy found the book he was looking for and waved it at Zach. "Read me the story."

Andy brought the book over to the sofa, sitting down close to Zach.

"Mr. Lightning might not have time." Jenny wished Andy wasn't so intent on relating to the cowboy. She supposed Andy would be that way with any man these days. But a drifter like Zach would have no patience with a little boy, and she couldn't bear to see Andy hurt. "He's resting."

Andy put his book down easily and looked at Zach with round eyes. "Is he sick?"

Zach heard Jenny's quick intake of breath at the same time as he saw the worry flare in Lisa's eyes as she stood next to her mother. Then he remembered what Charley had said about Jenny's husband dying of cancer. "Don't worry. I'm not the kind of guy who gets sick. I'm healthy as a horse."

"Your horse is sick," Lisa reminded him as she walked over to the sofa and stood on the other side of Zach.

"That's just Thunder's disposition," Zach said. He couldn't help but notice how the girl came close to him, but not too close. "He just likes to complain about his aches and pains. He's not a sunshine kind of guy like me."

Zach saw the quick smile that crossed Lisa's face before she rolled her eyes.

"My daddy got sick," Andy said quietly as he snuggled closer to Zach's side. "He died."

Jenny caught her breath. This was the first time either one of the kids had mentioned their father's death.

"That's what people do," Lisa said, her voice flat. She sat down on the sofa next to Zach. "No need to cry about it."

Zach wished he were a smarter man. He looked over at Jenny, but she didn't seem capable of speech, either. So he looked down at Lisa. "It's always okay to cry when you're sad."

Zach moved his arm so there was room and Lisa scooted closer until his arm was around her.

Everyone was silent for a few minutes.

"Here, let me see that book," Zach held his hand out for the book Andy had picked up again. "No reason we can't all read it together. I've always wondered about wolves. Thought I might get one for a pet one of these days."

"Wolves aren't pets," Lisa informed him. She moved a little farther away from Zach until her back was straight and she was perched cautiously on the edge of the sofa. "They're dangerous animals."

Zach had no idea how it happened, but the wolf led to some ballerina Lisa was anxious for him to read about.

"She has a tiara," Lisa told him solemnly as she pointed to the shiny circle on the girl's head in the book. By this time, Lisa had snuggled close to his elbow again.

"She looks like a real princess," Zach agreed. Zach decided he liked being enclosed by the kids. Now if only Jenny would join them on the sofa.

Jenny sat on a folding chair and looked at the cowboy and her children. She could not remember a scene like this one in her whole life. Even if her late husband, Stephen, had unbent enough to relate to one of the kids, he never included them both at the same time. He had certainly never read to them.

Who was she kidding? Reading was only part of what Zach had done. He had listened to her children. Maybe now that they had started talking to him about Stephen's death, they would talk about it some more with her. Maybe her children would find healing on this farm, after all.

It was past bedtime for Andy, but Jenny let the time pass. If it wasn't that she thought she might destroy the moment by capturing it, she would take a picture of the three of them. Her children would remember this cowboy reading and talking to them for a long time.

"I asked Santa for a tiara," Lisa sighed as Zach finished reading the last page of the book. "But it's too expensive."

"Santa doesn't need money," Andy said cheerfully as he wiggled even closer to Zach. "He's got elves. They'll make you up one of those things."

"Elves can't make tiaras," Lisa said as she straightened her back and took the book out of Zach's hands. "They don't have any jewels. You need jewels for a tiara."

"Oh." Andy thought about this. "But they have cowboy stuff. Cowboy stuff doesn't take jewels. You could ask for some of that, like me."

Lisa stood up to take the book back to the box. "I hope you didn't write that in your letter. If I can't have a tiara, I at least want something that's pretty. I don't want anything cowboy."

Jenny knew what was coming and tried to head the question off before it was formed. "Time for bed, Andy." Jenny stood up and added another distraction. "You can wear your cowboy pajamas." Jenny kept her voice cheerful and calm, but she could see the frown forming on Andy's face.

"When are you going to take my letter to Santa, Mr. Lightning?" Andy asked in a soft voice. "Lisa said you had to bring her back. You never got to the North Pole."

Zach reached out automatically and patted the pocket that held the letter. Uh-oh. He'd forgotten it was still there. He looked to Jenny for help.

"Mr. Lightning did his best," Jenny said softly as she walked over to her son. "But there's a blizzard outside. The roads are all full of snow. He had to turn back before he got to the North Pole."

Andy looked up at Zach in alarm. "But you're still going to take my letter, aren't you? It's almost time for Santa to come. He has to get my letter or he won't know what to bring me."

Zach knew he was a sucker. There was no longer any doubt. "I'm just waiting for everyone to go to bed. Then I'll crank up the old truck and make a quick trip."

Andy looked up at Zach in relief. "It won't take long. You can go fast. Zoom, zoom. You said so."

"That I did."

Lisa rolled her eyes and Jenny opened her mouth to protest, but neither of them said anything.

"The quicker you get to bed, the sooner I can get going to the North Pole," Zach said.

Jenny had never seen her son so anxious to get to bed. Andy ran into his room and changed into his pajamas in the thin streaks of light that shone into his room from the living room. Even Lisa seemed content to go to her bedroom. Jenny had managed to get a single mattress for each of the bedrooms, but she hadn't prepared for company. "I'm sorry, I don't have a guest room or anything."

Zach smiled. "That's all right. I think I

better sleep out in the barn and keep the fire going for that cat."

"At least there's a bed out there," Jenny said. "And I know the children will be glad you kept the cat warm."

"I don't suppose the beast has a name," Zach asked. He'd seen a white face looking at him from behind a stall, but he hadn't gotten close to the cat.

"She's not ours to name."

"She's living in your barn."

"Well, still—maybe she belongs somewhere else."

"She probably belongs to Mrs. Groussley. The cat probably wanted some solitude."

Jenny walked over to a box and pulled out several wool blankets. "I have some blankets, of course, that you can use. I don't have a spare pillow, but we can roll a blanket up and—"

"I'll be fine," Zach said.

Jenny had been worrying. The Santa letter had become more complicated than she'd ever imagined. "Andy can be persistent."

"That's a good thing."

Jenny kept her voice low as she gave the blankets to Zach. "We'll just tell him in the morning that you went to Santa's while he was asleep."

"You think he'll believe that?" Zach whispered in amazement. "If I know him, he's going to lie awake in there until he hears me leave." Zach shook his head in pride. "He might only be four, but he's awfully sharp."

"But what else can we do?"

Zach no longer bothered to lower his voice. "In just a few minutes, I'm going to go out to my truck and start driving it away."

"Oh." Jenny knew she shouldn't have expected him to stay. "I see."

Jenny swallowed before it occurred to her that even if the man wasn't the kind who stayed around, he didn't look like the kind who was crazy enough to head back to the main road in this weather.

"There's a blizzard out there," she whispered just in case he had forgotten. "You won't get halfway to Dry Creek without getting stuck."

"Ah." Zach smiled and winked at her. "But I don't need to get to Dry Creek. I only need to get to the North Pole."

They both heard the sigh of deep contentment that came from Andy's room before they heard the boy's voice. "It won't take long."

"No, it won't, partner," Zach agreed as he stood up. "It won't take long at all."

"Mom can go with you," Andy offered from

the bedroom. "Just in case you get lost on the way back. She knows the way back here real good."

Now that's an idea, Zach thought to himself, before he realized how unlikely that would be with the kids in bed. "Your mom probably needs to stay with you."

Zach glanced sideways at Jenny just in case she was the kind of mother who was willing to leave her kids alone on a dark night so she could go for a freezing-cold drive with a bachelor.

Zach had known women who would have left their kids in strip joints if it meant they could spend time with a cowboy. Not that he was passing judgment on those women. He knew plenty of men who were just as irresponsible. Who was he fooling? He was one of those men who were just as irresponsible.

"It sure would keep me warmer if I had some company," Zach said softly as he followed Jenny out into the kitchen. If Jenny was the kind of mother willing to leave her kids, she'd be the kind of woman to give him a friendly kiss or two out there under the night sky. He had a sudden, powerful urge to know if her wide blue eyes changed colors and danced with stars when she was kissed. "I wonder how cold it is out there, anyway."

"Give me a minute and I'll let you know.
I've gotten pretty accurate at guessing temperature." Jenny turned back to look at Zach.

Zach stepped closer. He wondered if Jenny
could tell how much the kitchen had heated up
since she'd turned to face him. He knew his
temperature had risen by ten degrees. Her face
was dusted with pink. And it was from more
than the red in the lights on his belt. The kitchen
was still in shadows but her face looked petal
soft. He could almost taste those kisses. He
figured her for a sweet kisser. He couldn't wait
to find out just how sweet.

It took a second or two for Zach to get past
his thoughts of kissing and realize Jenny was
willing to leave the kids and go off with him for
a long ride into the night. It took another
second for his disappointment to settle. He'd
have wagered his saddle that she was a better
parent than that. Not that his disappointment
would stop him from showing the lady a good
time, he told himself. "It doesn't matter how
cold it is out there, I'll keep you warm."

Now that Zach realized Jenny wasn't a saint,
he figured the same old lines would work with
her that he'd used in the rodeo for years. He
was back in the game.

Jenny rolled her eyes, but didn't even respond

to him. She just turned and walked toward the far kitchen wall. "I hope you don't mind if I drive the postal truck. The kids will be fine with you here."

"What?" Zach couldn't believe it. He was still stuck in his fantasy of her warm lips in the cold night. What had she said? He followed her through the kitchen. "You're going without me? Without *me?* Out there—into that blizzard?"

Was the woman crazy?

"Do you know how cold it is out there?" he asked, just to be sure. "It isn't anyplace for a woman alone—not on a night like tonight. This wind chill is nothing to mess around with—especially for a woman alone."

Zach knew he had said the wrong thing even as he saw Jenny bristle. She turned to face him.

"Actually—" Jenny's voice was chilly enough to match the outdoors "—a woman alone is just fine—inside or outside. Especially if she's read her guidebooks. The fact is women are better suited for the cold than men."

Zach lifted his eyebrow.

Jenny put her chin up in the air slightly. "It's true. It's because of body fat. Women have more body fat."

"But only in—" Zach stopped. He wasn't

sure Jenny would like him to tell her where her body fat was stored. Especially since it was in places that were causing him some discomfort now that the idea of kissing her had taken hold of him with a vengeance. Maybe he was the one who was crazy here.

Jenny turned and reached up to the coat hooks that were next to the door. "Well, we can't both go." Jenny lifted a drab blanket that was hanging on the hook. She'd grown accustomed to being both mother and father to her children years ago. "I wouldn't expect a stranger to do this for my children. It's my responsibility. Besides, I should have gotten the letter to Santa some other way before you came. It's not your problem."

The kitchen windows all looked out at the black night. Zach took a breath.

"It might not be my problem, but it is my truck." Zach put his hands on his hips. Let her argue with that. "I'll drive the thing."

"You hate that truck. You said so earlier." Jenny wrapped the blanket around her shoulders like a shawl. "Besides, we both know it's not your truck. It belongs to the people of Dry Creek. I know all about the mail service around here. And I *am* one of the people of Dry Creek, so it's more mine than yours."

"That truck is entrusted to my care," Zach said stubbornly. He'd moved his hands away from his hips. The extra Santa padding under that suit he still wore made him feel ridiculous. "Charley didn't say anything about me lending it out to folks to go driving around in it like it's some kind of do-it-yourself taxicab."

"I'm a good driver." Jenny held out her hand for the keys. "You can wait in the kitchen until I get back so the kids think you're gone, too. Just keep an eye on that furnace."

"Well, if they think I'm gone, maybe I should be."

"Somebody needs to be here in case something goes wrong." Jenny flashed Zach a smile. "Don't worry—the kids won't be a problem. They don't come out of their beds once they get settled. That's one good thing about it being cold. They don't want to leave their bed once they get the sheets warm."

Zach's frown turned to a scowl. Speaking of sheets, something was wrong with that blanket Jenny was holding like a shawl. "Is that what you use for a coat?"

Jenny lifted her chin as she wrapped the blanket more closely around her shoulders. "We used to live in Los Angeles. It wasn't cold enough there to need heavy coats."

"Well, this isn't Los Angeles." Zach looked at the other two hooks. They both held new snow coats, one in pink for Lisa and one in red for Andy. "You should have bought a coat for yourself when you bought the ones for the kids."

Jenny shrugged. "The kids needed the coats more than I did. I can get by until spring."

Zach didn't say anything. Boy, was he wrong to think she was an irresponsible parent. She was halfway to sainthood. Which made him proud in a funny sort of a way. Until he figured it out. If she was that kind of woman, his odds of getting a free kiss in this house were about the same as they would be at a PTA meeting filled with Republican grandmothers.

He'd learned long ago that kissing good women was complicated. They tended to take their kissing seriously. A kiss or two and they started thinking about china patterns and meeting your family. Zach didn't even know where his parents were anymore. Even if he did know, he sure wasn't going to take any woman to meet them.

Jenny lifted the blanket up to wrap it around her head as well as her shoulders.

"Andy asked me to deliver his letter." Zach pulled up the collar on his Santa suit. His hopes of a kiss might be gone, but he still would do this his way. "I'm responsible for the U.S. mail. I'm the one who's going."

Jenny looked at the man. The kitchen was in shadows, but she had no problem seeing the face before her. Faint red lines marked his cheek where the Santa beard had rubbed. A strong chin was brushed lightly with late-day whiskers. Brown eyes met hers with determination. She'd seen that same steady look in his eyes in rodeo pictures of him on those cereal boxes. He made one fierce-looking Santa.

"But it's cold out there."

"Then make me something hot to drink when I get back." Zach reached for the knob on the door. He wasn't going to argue on this one. He wouldn't be able to think straight if he let her take off in a night blizzard while he stayed in the kitchen. What kind of man would he be if he did that?

"I don't know what to say," Jenny tried again. The blanket around her shoulders was stiff, but she held it firm. "You shouldn't have to do this. You don't even like Christmas."

"Yes, I do." Zach gritted his teeth. What was it about this family? "I just don't see the need to go overboard and fuss about everything."

"You mean fuss about things like delivering a child's letter to Santa?" Jenny asked softly.

"Well, no. The letter, now that's important U.S. Postal Service business. I'm just doing my job."

Jenny smiled. "You're losing money. There's not even an official stamp on the envelope."

"It's official enough for me." He paused and added, "Besides, I gave my word. He's counting on me."

Jenny was speechless, and Zach took that as sign enough to open the door and leave.

The cold outside air lingered briefly inside while Jenny stood at the door's window and watched the red and green lights bump their way down her driveway. So that's what this man did when he gave his word. He actually carried through with his promise.

All Jenny saw of the postal truck was lights. She could, of course, hear the truck. She suspected Zach revved the motor a little extra just so it was very obvious that he was driving away.

Jenny was amazed. This cowboy was actually honoring his word. Her late husband had only considered promises made to adults to be binding. And then only if the adults were other men. Jenny was beginning to wonder if she hadn't misjudged the cereal-box cowboy. Not that it would make much difference. A man with that much sexual magnetism was not the kind of man she wanted in her life the second time around.

If and when she married again, she would marry for the sake of her children. And she wouldn't take any chances. She'd marry a solid Christian man. Someone boring would be fine. She wasn't going to be deceived if she could help it. She'd make sure the man knew his Bible and prayed. She didn't think Zach had ever even opened a Bible. He sure hadn't looked comfortable earlier when they'd prayed.

Jenny pulled the blanket closer around her shoulders as though she could press the heat into her skin. She wished the cowboy had let her make the drive. She felt beholden enough to him already and didn't relish adding a favor like this to the list. She had her pride. She just had no way to repay him.

Unless—Jenny still had a few dollars in the bank. She could write him a check. Yes, a check, she thought to herself in satisfaction. A check should even the score nicely.

Outside in the cold, Zach stopped the postal truck. He'd driven a quarter of a mile away from the house when he stopped and turned out the lights, just in case Andy had watched him leave the house. He'd leave the lights off for a few minutes so that it would look like the truck was far, far away on its way to the North Pole. He knew Jenny had said that the kids both stayed tucked into bed once they were down, but he also knew that Christmas changed the rules for kids everywhere.

Without the heater on, the temperature inside the postal truck dipped quickly. If Jenny had been sitting next to him, Zach knew he'd ask her what the temperature was just to challenge her skill. He smiled. She was some amazing lady. He wondered if she really could tell temperatures like that.

The black night, even with the cold outside, was peaceful. Zach clicked on the lights on his belt so he could read his watch. He'd had the lights off for five minutes. He wondered how long a kid would figure it would take to go to the North Pole.

Speaking of the North Pole, Zach pulled out the letter Andy had written. He wasn't curious about what the requests were. The kids had already told him what they wanted. But he was beginning to worry.

The box he'd brought out to this family hadn't been heavy enough to satisfy any child's Santa wish. Besides, he knew what was in it.

The camera, a frozen ham that Jenny had already put in the unheated laundry room, the pie from Mrs. Hargrove, and two small brown bags from some store in Miles City.

Those brown bags looked awfully puny.

Zach sat in silence. He knew firsthand how it felt to be disappointed at Christmas. He'd never believed in Santa Claus, but when he was ten years old someone had sent his parents a Christmas card with a family picture on the front of it. Everyone in the picture was standing beside a Christmas tree and looking happy. That was Zach's first glimpse of what the day was like for other families, and that Christmas Zach had decided it should be that way for his family.

Zach had begged a scrawny leftover tree from a nearby lot on Christmas Eve and set it up in the living room. He'd thought a tree would make the difference. He'd believed the tree would turn his family into a Christmas family like the one on that card. But his parents had only used the tree as an excuse to drink more than usual, quarreling over who should propose the next toast to the greenery.

No one in his family smiled that Christmas, and Zach threw the tree away the next day. That was the last time he had had any hopes at

Christmas. But he'd never spent Christmas with children like Andy and Lisa. They were good kids. They deserved a good Christmas.

Zach did not know exactly when in the darkness the idea came to him, but it somehow did. He, Zach "Lightning" Lucas, knew what the children wanted. They knew that he wasn't the real Santa but they had still both trusted him with their Christmas wishes. Maybe it was time Zach lived up to the red suit he wore. In this snow-covered corner of Montana he was Santa. He would see that their hoped-for presents were delivered.

At first Zach thought about driving into Dry Creek tomorrow, but then he realized he had the same limitations that had faced Jenny. The hardware store in Dry Creek would not have either Lisa's tiara or Andy's cowboy outfit. Besides, the roads wouldn't be open, anyway. And he was driving a postal truck, not a bull-dozer.

Of course, the cowboy outfit—Zach looked into the back of the postal truck. His duffel bag was still there along with his sheepskin coat. He hadn't packed much for his trip to Vegas, but he did have the latest championship buckle in there that he had just won last month. He knew how to work with leather and he had a broken bridle in his duffel that he'd been meaning to fix. He might be able to fashion a belt for the boy. And he could put a thick lining in his spare Stetson hat to fit the kid. He didn't have a toy gun, but he could make a small rope with some of that postal twine in the truck.

Lisa's tiara would be more difficult. Especially because, as she'd reminded Andy, a tiara needed to have jewels. Zach grinned to himself. Now that he thought of it, he did have jewels. Zach reached into the back and pulled the duffel toward him. He unzipped the bag and felt around in the contents until his hand found what he was seeking. He'd brought a Christmas present for Patti.

He twirled the lacy leg garter on his finger and grinned. The showgirl would never miss the fancy garter he'd bought her. But Lisa would love the rhinestones that circled it. There were pink rhinestones and clear rhinestones and small pieces of real ruby. And, if Jenny had a metal clothes hanger that he could bend, he'd be in business.

By the time Zach turned the engine back on in the postal truck, he'd decided that this Christmas might be tolerable after all. Imagine Zach "Lightning" Lucas filling in for Santa Claus.

Zach said "ho ho ho" to himself just to see if he had the knack.

He didn't.

But that didn't matter. Zach would pretend to have the Christmas spirit even if it killed him. He'd do it for the sake of the kids.

He only hoped Jenny would cooperate.

## Chapter Six

Jenny looked out the window again. It had been totally black outside the last time she'd peeked, but now she could see the lights of the postal truck coming closer to the house. Jenny was beginning to have second thoughts. She'd looked at her bank book and the crude budget she'd worked up to see them through the winter, before deciding to write the check for seven dollars. It wasn't much, but it was all she dared give away until she knew how much it would cost to fix the radiator on her car.

The truck engine came to a stop near the house, and Jenny smoothed back her hair. She'd put some water into her fondue pan and lit the candle underneath. She didn't know how long it would take the water to heat, but she intended to have a hot drink for Zach when he came inside. That and the check would make her feel less indebted to him.

Zach sat in the postal truck. While he was driving back up the path that led to Jenny's house, he'd noticed the ball of mistletoe someone had hung on the antenna of the truck. It would freeze solid if he left it outside over night. He might as well haul it in with his gear.

Zach opened the door and stepped outside into the snow.

The night was kinder to Jenny's house than the light of day had been. In the dark, the flickering light through the kitchen window gave the house a warm look, as if someone was waiting up for the last one of the family to come home.

Maybe, Zach thought wryly, that's why he preferred busy hotels. With all the neon flash of a hotel at night, everyone knew there was nothing personal about the fact that someone was waiting up inside. It was strictly business. Zach liked it that way. If no one was waiting up, there would never be anyone disappointed after discovering that Zach knew absolutely nothing about the things other people took for granted.

The Christmas tree failure had been only one of the lessons he'd learned as a child. It was that same year he'd discovered other families ate their meals together at a table. He'd asked his mother if they could do the same. One meal together had cured them all of the idea. His family wouldn't even have a clue what to do when Jenny's children had bowed their heads earlier today to pray.

No, Zach knew he wasn't meant for family life. He doubted God wanted someone like him saying prayers to Him on a regular basis, anyway. That was best left to church-going folks.

Of course, there was no need for him to even think about such things, Zach told himself with a shake of his head. He'd made peace with his limitations many years ago. He wouldn't wish the life he'd had growing up on anyone, but that was what he knew. Zach figured he was destined to follow in his parents' footsteps, and it wasn't a path he wanted anyone else to have to walk with him.

Besides, he was fine with being alone. The rodeo life was a good life, even if the thrill of it had grown decidedly thin in the past few years. Maybe next year he'd see about having some kind of a home base. He didn't mind washing his own socks, but he sure did miss a steady drawer to put them in.

Still, rodeo riding was what he knew and what he was good at. No one expected anything from him in the rodeo world that he did not know exactly how to give them. That should be enough for any man, he told himself as he reached Jenny's door.

Zach stamped his feet lightly outside the door, shaking the snow off them. He wore his heavy coat over the Santa suit and carried the mistletoe in one hand and his duffel bag in the other.

"What the…?" Zach muttered to himself as the mistletoe pricked him. The spikes on the holiday weed were big enough that the whole thing should be declared a lethal weapon. Zach half hung the mistletoe on his coat pocket and reached for the doorknob before he hesitated.

Polite manners were never his strong suit. But he figured even if the light in the window was for him, he was still company in this house and would be expected to knock rather than just come inside as though he belonged here. No matter how tempted he was to do just that, it wasn't right. He didn't belong. So he knocked.

The window on the door was frosted over, but the light from inside shone through the iced pattern.

"Come in," Jenny called softly from inside the kitchen.

Jenny had decided payment of a debt

required some special touches. She brought down two cups and saucers from her good china set. She'd even put a lace cloth on the folding table. That should be enough, Jenny thought to herself when she heard Zach on the porch. The tea and the check should bring them about even.

When he opened the door, however, Jenny decided she should have forgotten the tea and left the check until the morning. She should have done whatever was necessary to be as far away from this man as was possible in her old house. The cold had turned the man into someone who looked as if he belonged on one of those calendars for single women. He was Mr. December.

Jenny shivered all the way down her spine. She told herself it was because of the cold wind that blew into the kitchen in the quick second before Zach turned to close the door.

But it wasn't.

Just look at him, she thought in dismay. Zach was the kind of man she had moved a thousand miles to avoid. Montana men were supposed to be farmers. Steady, reliable men with faces one learned to love. She wasn't supposed to meet a man like Zach, whose face would make a young girl swoon. But there he stood against the black of the night like some mountain man covered with snow.

The kitchen was dark except for the half dozen candles Jenny had lit, some on the counter and some on the table in the middle of the kitchen. The candlelight made the snow scattered over Zach's dark hair glisten like confetti. The cold had turned his skin to marble. His brown eyes simmered beneath strong brows, and snow had settled on his eyebrows. More snow had fallen on the shoulders of his heavy leather coat as it hung from his frame.

In that long coat, all hints of a friendly Santa were covered.

"Thanks for waiting up," Zach said as he stood on the rug by the kitchen door and set his duffel on the floor nearby. "It was nice of you."

Jenny was speechless. Then she decided the best way to deal with the situation was to meet it rationally.

"It wasn't long." Jenny took a deep breath and walked closer to him as he tried to get his arm out of his coat. If she could only get that coat off him, she'd be fine. She could cope with a man dressed as Santa. "Here, let me help you with that."

Zach stopped in surprise. He couldn't remember the last time anyone had offered to help him with anything. He'd always had to fend for himself. "I can get it."

"Not with that Santa suit on under your coat. Believe me, I know. Andy has a playsuit out of that fuzzy material, and it's almost impossible for one person to get the coat pulled off the sleeves."

"Oh."

Zach was pretty sure Jenny was wrong, but he hoped she didn't discover the fact. She had moved so close that he could inhale the pure soap smell of her.

Jenny gripped the edge of Zach's coat sleeve and tugged.

"Something's caught." Jenny pulled on the sleeve again before looking up at Zach.

Jenny looked back down at the sleeve. Looking up was a mistake. She needed to keep focused on the Santa material. Polyester. That wasn't sexy. Think of Andy's playsuit. "It'll come off in a minute."

Zach wasn't paying any attention to her words. He wondered if she knew what the candlelight did to her blond hair. She'd combed the short curls back and had them clipped with some combs. But little wisps of hair escaped here and there, making it look as if she wore a halo.

Zach caught his breath. His skin was still cold from outside, but Jenny slipped her hand inside the sleeve of his coat and his skin warmed up in a hurry.

"Andy's coat never did this." Jenny bit her lip as she frowned up at Zach.

"Huh?" Zach stopped breathing as her hands slid farther under the Santa suit and up his forearm. Her hands were soft as an angel's beneath the weight of both the Santa suit and his sheepskin coat.

"Ouch!" Jenny said.

"Ouch!" Zach said.

The ball of mistletoe dropped to the floor and rolled.

"Sorry. I forgot I'd hung that halfway in my pocket."

"It's mistletoe."

Zach noticed Jenny didn't sound any too happy about the fact.

"It was on the truck antenna. I think Charley put it there," Zach said.

Jenny nodded curtly. The old men of Dry Creek were all matchmakers. They'd put mistletoe on a hearse just in case the corpse met anyone on the way to his own funeral.

"I couldn't just leave the stuff outside. It'd freeze." Zach bent down and gingerly picked

the mistletoe up by the string that had tied it to
the antenna. "Besides, it is a Christmas deco-
ration. Thought you might be able to use it."

"I guess we could put it in the laundry room,"
Jenny offered after a moment. After all, the old
men did mean well. "With the ham."

"What's a ham need with a wad of mistletoe
like ours?"

"Ours?" Jenny looked up at him quizzically.
The shadows in the kitchen left her eyes in
darkness. Zach wished he could see them
more clearly. Her eyes gave away her
emotions, and he felt that he was flying blind
when he couldn't see them.

"Well, you know—you and the kids," Zach
stammered, before he added himself to the list.
Man, this woman made him nervous. "You
don't need to worry about it being mistletoe. I
mean, with the kissing and all. It's not like I'm
planning to kiss you."

Jenny blinked. She wasn't planning to kiss
him, either. Of course not. "Good…that's good."

It was good they understood each other. Very
good. She would have had to speak to him if
he intended to kiss her, too, assure him that
they had no prospects. That would have been
awkward, and she was glad there was no need
to do it. But still…

"Not that I don't want to kiss you." Zach threw that in for good measure. Jenny still wasn't smiling. "Any man would want to kiss you. I mean, you're very, ah, pleasant. Very pleasant."

Jenny frowned slightly. "Pleasant" sounded like someone's grandmother. No wonder he was stuttering and stammering all over the place. Apparently she wouldn't have had to speak to him at all. "You don't want to kiss me."

"Huh?"

"Not that it's a problem," Jenny chattered. When she was upset, she always talked too much. "Which is for the best. Of course. In fact, you shouldn't even think about it. I mean, there's no need—I mean, well, you're just snowed in for Christmas. Snowbound really. We're not even each other's type—I mean, it's not like we're—that is—you just brought the mail and I'm grateful for that."

Sometimes a man had to gamble with his life, Zach thought. Sometimes he even had to gamble with his heart.

Zach bent down and kissed Jenny.

Or at least he thought he did. Maybe she was the one who tilted her head back and arched up to meet his lips. He would never know. All he knew was that he was kissing Jenny.

Zach had never expected the rush of pure sweetness to be followed by a hint of fire. That was his only excuse for lingering over the kiss.

Jenny stood rooted to the floor. She knew it was a mistake to kiss this cowboy, knew it when she'd told herself to step back and then found herself unable to do it. What was wrong with her, anyway? She usually had more sense. Something was wrong with her. It was...

"Christmas," Jenny whispered the word to herself as if it were a lifeline. Of course. It must be because of the holiday that she was letting this man kiss her senseless. That was it. The holiday.

People did strange things at holidays. They ate fruitcake. Rang old metal bells. They even forgot their very sensible vows and kissed good-looking cowboys who were just passing through.

"Hmm." Zach smoothed back Jenny's hair. "What about Christmas?"

"It's making me crazy." Jenny tried to collect herself. What was that purring in the back of her mind? "Well, not just me—both of us—Christmas and mistletoe. You know, it's crazy."

Zach didn't like this line of thought. "Christmas doesn't make people go crazy."

Kisses like the one they'd just shared might make people go crazy, Zach conceded to himself, but a date on the calendar never would. He'd missed out on a lot of things about Christmas, but crazy wasn't one of them.

"Of course it does." Jenny stepped farther back and kept chatting. Even her teeth were nervous around this man. She was lucky she wasn't blabbing. "There's the Santa fantasy. Every kid gets carried away with Santa. Even when we're adults we expect the, well, unusual at Christmas."

"You think us kissing is about Christmas?"

Zach's voice was quiet, but Jenny didn't stop. She couldn't stop.

"Well, you know the goodwill, peace toward men—that kind of thing."

"I see." Zach turned slightly and, even with one hand holding the mistletoe string, pulled his arm away from his coat sleeve. A slight buzz of static filled the silence. So that's why Jenny had kissed him—goodwill? A man certainly couldn't go very far with that. A woman kissed her uncle for goodwill, or a child. She probably got extra points for cozying up to a sick orphan.

"It didn't mean anything. The kiss, I mean," Jenny stammered. The man was scowling about something. She supposed it was the kiss. He was experiencing after-kiss remorse. She'd seen it before. "We were just—"

"I know—" Zach hung his coat on one of the hooks and tried to stop scowling "—crazy at Christmas."

"Yeah."

Zach could vouch for the fact that at least one of them was crazy. The bottom had sure fallen out of his stability. And people wondered why he wasn't overly fond of the holiday.

Jenny shook herself. "It was only a kiss." And a tidal wave is only a little water, she mocked herself. She felt as if she'd jumped into the deep end before she'd learned to swim. She'd never meant to be this vulnerable again. And him, he was only passing through on his way to— "You were just lonesome for your friend."

"Huh?"

"The showgirl."

"Oh, Cathy."

"I thought you said her name was Patti."

Zach didn't like the way Jenny was looking at him—as though he was such a roving cowboy that he didn't even remember names. "It is Patti. I just call her Cathy sometimes."

Now she'd think he was certifiable, for sure. Zach assured himself the only reason he couldn't remember names was because Jenny was making him nervous. Usually he did fine.

Jenny continued chatting. "Speaking of your trip…" She willed herself to stop, but it did no good. She didn't even want to think about his trip to Las Vegas. She surely didn't want to talk about it. "You'll be needing some money."

"What?" Did she think he was paying for it? "Patti's a showgirl, but she's not—I mean, she doesn't charge."

Zach wondered if she thought he was so unattractive he needed to pay for it. She'd already made it clear she didn't particularly like his looks. But to say that—well, it was pretty discouraging when he'd just kissed her.

"I meant for gas. You'll need to buy gas to get there." Jenny willed her mind to focus. There she'd gone and insulted his girlfriend. And him, too, she supposed. "All I mean to say is that I have a check for you."

"Gas money?" Zach repeated in disbelief. He wondered if the woman knew how much money he had in his bank account. When he compared it with what was probably in hers, he was speechless. He could buy her miserable little farm a dozen times over and still have change. "I don't need gas money."

"Well, you'll need something someday—and you've done so much for us tonight." Jenny made the mistake of looking up directly into

Zach's eyes. She'd heard of eyes that smoldered, but she'd never actually seen any that did until now. He was angry. The gold in his eyes sparked until it melted the brown. She completely forgot what she was going to say.

"You don't owe me anything."

"Still." Jenny gathered herself together. She needed to be strong for her children. She walked over to the counter and picked up the check. "I don't want to be beholden."

Zach saw the cornered pride in Jenny's eyes. So that was it. His face softened. "You're not beholden. You've offered me shelter in a storm. That's worth more than some ride in the dark."

"But it's just a bunk in the barn."

"I've slept on worse. Many nights."

Jenny held out the check. "I'd still feel better if you took this."

Zach didn't want to take her check. Of course, it probably didn't make any difference since he'd never cash it. "I guess."

Zach reached out to take the check with one hand. The other hand held tight to the mistletoe string.

The kitchen was quiet except for the tick of the battery-operated clock on the wall. The candles carved out pockets of golden light by the counters and the table in the middle of the room.

Zach heard a shuffle in the corner and a yawn. Come to think of it, he'd heard the shuffle for some time now. He wondered how long the little feet had been standing there.

"Mama, it's too late to give Santa a letter." Andy's voice came from the doorway to the kitchen. "Mr. Lightning, you already took the letters to Santa Claus, didn't you?"

Andy padded over to Zach and wrapped his arms around one of Zach's thighs. "You're cold."

Zach was surprised the cold didn't stop Andy from hugging his leg. "It was cold out there— going to the North Pole."

Zach let his hand rest on the boy's head.

"You should be in bed," Jenny gently scolded. Jenny didn't like the fact that her son had gone to the cowboy instead of her for the third time tonight.

"But Santa won't get your letter," Andy said worriedly as he looked up at his mother. He didn't leave his post by Zach's leg as he pointed to the check Zach held in his hand.

"That wasn't a letter. It was a check." Jenny hoped her son's fascination with the cowboy didn't turn to tears when the man left.

"Santa doesn't need a check."

"No, the check was for Mr. Lucas." Jenny hoped the formal title would remind Zach that just because her son wrapped himself around his leg at every opportunity he got it did not mean they were anything but strangers.

"It should have been a list," Andy protested. "What you want from Santa."

"Santa doesn't come to mommies," Jenny said.

Andy's eyes grew wide. "Because they've been bad?"

Jenny smiled. "No, it's just that Santa is special for little kids."

"But won't you get any presents?" Andy was frowning as he clutched Zach's leg even harder. "You've gotta have a present."

"Of course she'll have a present." Zach frantically thought about what else might be in his duffel bag that could be made into a present for Jenny. No wonder Santa was fat. The stress of thinking of all those Christmas gifts would drive anyone to eating too many cookies. "I just don't know what yet."

"We could give her the Christmas ball," Andy announced as he pointed to the mistletoe that hung from Zach's other hand. "I've seen those. They're for kisses. Mommy likes kisses."

"She does?" Zach watched the pink sweep across Jenny's face. "Now isn't that nice."

Andy nodded happily. "I kiss her every night and she sleeps with my kiss under her pillow."

"She does?"

Andy nodded as he pretended to scoop a kiss out of the air. "I blow one to her so she can catch it."

"Isn't that nice." Zach wasn't at all in favor of that kind of kissing. Not when it came to Jenny. Of course, the pillow part sounded nice.

Andy squeezed Zach's leg tighter. "Is Mommy going to keep your kiss under her pillow tonight?"

Zach heard Jenny's gasp.

"Mommy, ah…" Zach jumped in to explain before Jenny could deny everything. He knelt down so he was facing Andy directly. "Your mommy only has room under her pillow for kisses from her little boy. You give her special kisses."

Andy nodded happily. "I blow them to her."

Zach nodded. "That makes them easier for her to catch."

Andy leaned closer to Zach and whispered into his right ear, "I could teach you how to make special kisses. Then you could blow some to Mommy, too."

Jenny didn't like seeing the two heads together. Plus she couldn't hear what her son was saying. She didn't want to spoil Andy's illusions about the cowboy, but she didn't like him sharing his innocent thoughts with the man. "What's the secret?"

"Nothing." Zach knew Jenny wouldn't like what her son was saying.

Her son had no such hesitation. "I was just telling Mr. Lightning how to give you kisses that you keep under your pillow."

Jenny blushed.

"You should be back in bed," Jenny reminded her son. "It's cold out here."

"Tomorrow night Santa comes," Andy said blissfully as he continued to hug Zach's leg. "We're going to make cookies for Santa tomorrow, aren't we?"

Zach wondered when he'd become such a sucker for little boys. Maybe it was when they offered to teach him how to kiss their mothers. "Sure enough."

"I can stir," Andy offered proudly.

"You'll do a fine job," Jenny said firmly. "But first, you need to go to bed and sleep."

Andy yawned as he let go of Zach's leg and walked back out of the kitchen. "Good night, Mr. Lightning. Tell the kitty good night, too. I hope she stays warm in the barn."

"Good night. And don't worry about your kitty. I'll keep the fire going."

Zach watched Andy go. Now there was a

sweet little boy, full of hope and enthusiasm. He had to be, to think of that wild cat as a kitty. The thing was closer to a mountain cat. "His father must have been something."

"What?" Jenny looked up at Zach in alarm. Now where had that come from? She never talked about her husband. She'd not even told Mrs. Hargrove about Stephen. At first, she'd never told anyone about Stephen because she kept intending to talk to him first. But then he was sick. And now she felt it was disloyal to voice her disappointment about someone who was dead and couldn't make any changes, anyway. "What about Stephen?"

"To have raised a boy like Andy, he must have been a good father is all."

Zach was surprised at the surge of envy he felt. It must have felt good to be a man like Stephen and have something steady and loving to give to a wife and kids.

Jenny bit her lip. "Stephen wasn't well."

"I heard…the cancer." Zach could have kicked himself. Jenny's face had gone closed and pale. What kind of a brute was he, bringing back painful memories? "I'm sorry. You must miss him."

Jenny nodded. That was the sore truth of it. Even though he had kept to himself, she missed him. She had loved Stephen. For years. He had been her chosen one. She'd been hopeful. She'd prayed. She'd bargained for his attention. She'd lived expecting the day would come when Stephen would look around himself and realize the value of his family. That day had never come. She always felt there had been some trigger in Stephen that she hadn't been able to find. Something she should have known that had eluded her.

Zach called himself ten kinds of a fool. "I should be telling you about my trip to the frozen north instead of stirring up sad memories—especially at Christmas."

"And I should be offering you a cup of tea." Jenny gestured to the table. "And thanking you for making this Christmas a better one for my children."

Zach tried not to notice that she didn't include herself. "The Santa stuff was all Mrs. Brown's idea."

"Do you like your tea plain or with lemon?" Jenny walked back to the fondue pot. "I'm afraid it will only be a tea bag in a cup. I couldn't get enough water to heat to make a pot."

"A cup will be more than fine."

Jenny poured him a cup of tea in silence and

took it to the table. "I'm sure you'll enjoy some peace and quiet while you drink this."

Zach could have told her that he'd lived his life with peace and quiet. It wasn't what it was cracked up to be. But he didn't. She was rattled. He hoped she'd sit down at the table with him and have a cup of tea, as well.

"The tea smells good," Zach offered. "If you don't have enough water for two cups, I could get by with a half cup."

There. He'd asked her to share.

Jenny shook her head. "It's cold out there. You'll need your whole cup. Besides, I think I'm going to head to bed. Do you need anything else for the barn?"

"No, I'm fine. I already made the bed up with the blankets you gave me. I'll build a fire and it'll be fine."

"I know the cat will appreciate it."

Zach nodded. Of course, the cat. He watched Jenny walk out of the kitchen. "Good night."

Zach told himself he shouldn't mind. He was, after all, used to sitting at a table by himself and eating. He never even had a cat waiting up for him. It shouldn't bother him after all those years. He'd sat alone in coffee shops. In hotel rooms. In bars. He should be used to it. Zach looked around at the shadows in the empty kitchen. Yeah, he should be used to it by now.

Suddenly he had no appetite for the tea. He might as well go out to the barn and see about warming the place up for the cat.

Zach followed the rope out to the barn although he didn't actually need it. The snow had stopped swirling and he could see the barn clearly from the house once he had his flashlight pointed in the right direction. He opened the main door to the barn and waved his flashlight around when he entered. He figured that cat was as cautious about meeting people as he was. Neither one of them wanted to be caught unaware.

Zach heard a hiss from the area of the hay bales so he figured he'd announced his presence for the night. He then walked to the small room off to the right. He suspected the room he was sleeping in had been used by a series of hired men who had helped old man Collins before he died.

Zach had looked at the room when he was out here earlier and noticed there were odds and ends of things that had been left behind by others. An old razor—the metal kind from the sixties. A few Zane Grey westerns. An old Bible that looked like it'd been around for years. A couple of mugs and a blackened coffeepot on top of the wood stove.

Zach liked campfire coffee. He walked over to the wood stove and opened it up so he could build a fire. The metal was cold and the stove door creaked as it opened. He'd build a small fire tonight, but it would be enough to warm this room.

He heard the cat meow somewhere in the barn. It was hard to judge if the meow sounded closer than the hiss, but Zach thought so.

"Give me a minute, will ya?" Zach muttered. "It's going to take a minute to build us a fire worth anything."

Zach looked at the door to the room. He'd leave it partially open just in case the cat had sense enough to follow the heat closer to the fire. Not that the room would ever become comfortably warm with the door cracked like that.

Zach shook his head. He was going soft. The next thing he knew he'd be warming the cat's milk on that wood stove along with his morning coffee. He shook his head again.

## Chapter Seven

Jenny woke with her pillow twisted around her shoulders. She'd had a dream that there were hot coals hiding under her pillow, and it took a couple of deep breaths to assure herself that everything was all right. She could feel her cheeks were aflame even though the air around them was cool.

She let herself remember where she was. She was in the farmhouse, lying on the mattress in her bedroom. The faint light of daybreak streaked into the room through the gap between her drapes. The day looked subdued. It was probably cloudy outside. Most likely the electricity was still off. At least the wind had died down.

Jenny took a deep breath to calm herself. She was surprised at the sense of contentment she felt when she slowly realized where she was. She was home.

Jenny heard the quiet giggling before she even had a chance to turn over again. She couldn't mistake the sound of Andy's laughter, and it didn't take too many guesses to place the deeper tones. Zach.

Jenny wondered what she was going to do with her son. How did you tell a four-year-old that it wasn't wise to become attached to a man who was going to be gone in a couple of days?

Maybe you didn't, Jenny said to herself as she stood up and slipped on her robe. Maybe all she could do was distract Andy as much as possible so that he was busy with other things and stopped spending time with the cowboy.

Jenny looked at her face in the mirror on the back of her bedroom door and grimaced. Her blond hair was naturally curly, and this morning it was flyaway. Usually her hair was only like this when it was going to rain. She wasn't sure if her hair would react the same way to snow.

Fortunately, no one would notice her hair once they got a good look at her puffy eyes. She looked like someone who had been doing battle all night with her dreams. Too bad she was out of eyedrops.

She was a mess. But she wasn't in a beauty

contest today. All that mattered today was getting Christmas ready for her children. She, like her son, would do well to forget the cowboy was even here.

"Whoever gets the pan out of the cupboard gets the first pancake," Jenny announced firmly as she stepped into the living room.

Three pairs of eyes turned to her. She hadn't realized Lisa had joined the other two. Her two children were in their pajamas. The cowboy was dressed, of course. The three of them were huddled around something on the living room floor.

"Mama!" Lisa squeaked.

"Don't look," Andy added in panic.

The cowboy simply pulled the afghan off the sofa and spread it over something on the floor. "It's okay now."

Jenny eyed the afghan-covered lump on the floor. "What's that?"

"Well, now," the cowboy drawled. "That depends."

My goodness, Jenny thought as she looked at him closer. Didn't the man ever have a bad day? He looked just as pleased with himself as the children did. And his excitement made his brown eyes—well, it wouldn't do to look him in the eye for too long. "Depends on what?"

"Whether or not I tell you depends on whether you can keep a secret."

"She can't keep the secret. It's—" Lisa protested before she bit off her words and looked at Zach with reproach. "You're teasing."

Zach grinned back at Lisa. "Sure am."

Lisa smiled back before she rolled her eyes.

Jenny felt the need to sit down. Lisa never took to strangers. Granted, she'd run off to the North Pole with the man, but that was only to win a bet. Now Lisa was talking to him as if he were her best friend. Jenny wasn't sure she liked it. "You've got a secret?"

"Don't you know you're not supposed to ask questions at Christmas?" Zach finally said as he stood up.

Jenny was momentarily distracted. She thought rodeo cowboys were supposed to have aches and pains in every joint. Zach moved with a smoothness that made her mouth grow dry. If he ached anywhere it was unnoticeable. His whole body was a symphony of movements. Even his hair behaved. And that little dimple she sometimes glimpsed on his chin— Jenny stopped herself.

"Huh?" Jenny looked away from the cowboy and back at her children. They were sitting on the floor and both smiling at her.

"Oh, it's a Christmas something? For me?" Jenny finally understood. Now she was completely dumbfounded. Jenny couldn't remember the last time she had gotten a real present. She'd always bought herself some soap or bath gel and put "From Stephen" on the package at Christmas. When the children asked, she'd told them all she wanted was a kiss and a hug.

"It's a surprise," Andy said in satisfaction as he stood up and walked over to her. "From us."

"You'll like it," Lisa added confidently as she stood up. "But you can't see it. Not until you open it up on Christmas morning. We're going to put it under the Christmas tree."

"I wouldn't dream of peeking," Jenny said. She hadn't seen her children so excited for months. And Zach—the man stood square in the middle of their excitement, looking just as pleased as they were. "Your secret is safe. At least until Christmas morning."

"Christmas morning should have lots of surprises," Zach said. He looked almost as pleased as the children.

"Oh?" Jenny asked cautiously as she looked at him.

"I had company last night," Zach said in triumph.

Jenny gave a quick look at her two children.

She knew they were fascinated with the cowboy, but—

"The cat came inside my room," Zach continued. She had curled up right next to his boots. He had the stove door open and there was enough light so he could get a good look at the shape of her. "And I think she's going to have babies."

"Kittens! We're going to have kittens!" Lisa squealed as she stood up. "When?"

"Well, that's mostly up to the mama cat," Zach said. "But I think you're going to have a batch of Christmas kittens."

"We should at least move her onto the porch then," Jenny said. "The barn's no place for babies."

"Jesus was born in a barn," Andy said. "Remember? On Christmas Eve?"

"Well, yes, but that wasn't in a Montana blizzard," Jenny said. She had no idea how cold it had been in Bethlehem, but it couldn't have been twenty below.

"Oh," Andy said and was quiet for a minute. "We're going to read the story again, aren't we?"

"Of course we'll read the story," Jenny said. "We read it every Christmas."

Andy nodded. "Mr. Lightning can read it this time."

Zach went stiff. He wasn't even sure where the Christmas story was found. He knew it was in the Bible, but that was about it. "I'm not sure I—ah— That is—"

"We don't need to decide who reads the story yet," Jenny said. "We haven't even had breakfast."

"Where'd you say that frying pan is?" Zach asked in relief as he sat down on the sofa.

"Me first," Andy squealed as he ran out of the living room with Lisa following close behind him.

"Thanks," Zach said to Jenny when it was just the two of them left. "It's not that I wouldn't be happy to hear the story. It's just that—"

Jenny put her hand up. "I know Andy can be persistent sometimes."

"That's not a problem," Zach said. "The boy needs to be able to ask for things."

Jenny didn't answer, and Zach wondered if there was something else bothering her. She didn't look as happy now that the children were out of the room.

"I hope you don't mind us doing this," Zach said quietly as he gestured to the lump under the afghan. "Andy was already awake when I came inside this morning and we didn't want to wake you. It was early. So we had this idea of making a present. I didn't think to ask you. Maybe, as I think about it now, I should have gone in and woken you."

No, Zach said to himself, that wouldn't have been a good idea. The sight of Jenny all warm and curled up in her bed would not have been— well, it would not have been a good idea at all.

"Ah, no." Jenny felt her cheeks blush. She'd already had hot coals under her pillow this morning. "You don't need to ask permission. But Andy can be a handful."

"He's just excited. Christmas, you know. The crazy thing."

Jenny knew Christmas wasn't what was exciting Andy. It was having a grown man sit on the floor and pay attention to him.

"He's a good boy," Zach offered. He didn't want Jenny to think he minded spending time with Andy.

Zach had always liked children, but most of his encounters with kids were short and came about because the kid wanted his autograph or wanted to pet Thunder or something like that. He'd never had a chance to spend this much time with individual children like Andy and Lisa. He hadn't known what he was missing.

"I just don't want you to feel you need to

spend all of your time with the children. I know you don't like all the stuff that goes with holidays."

"I don't mind the children." What did she think he was? A monster? "It's only the holiday that I said that about—just the day on the calendar. Never the children. Children are supposed to like holidays."

"Oh." Jenny tried again. "Still, if you have other things to do—reading or something."

"The only books here are the children's books."

Jenny shrugged. "I thought maybe you brought something to read."

"I guess I could go check out the mailbag and see if I forgot to deliver any letters to Mrs. Goussley," Zach teased. What did she think? That he hauled around a library in his duffel bag?

Then it hit Zach, there were some books in the barn. But he didn't want to spend his time reading, anyway, so he kept quiet.

Jenny gave up. Stephen had always found some excuse to avoid spending time with the children. She figured she had given Zach enough excuses, he could pick one up anytime he wanted. She'd given him all the help she could.

"Unless—" Zach finally figured out what

was giving the woman heartburn "—unless you'd rather I not spend time with the kids."

"What?"

"I know some women think that a rodeo man might not know how to act around kids," Zach said, ignoring the fact that even he knew he didn't know how to act around kids. "But I've been watching my language. And I don't tell them anything that they shouldn't know about."

Zach almost mentioned that he hadn't even explained what a showgirl was when they'd asked again this morning. He'd let them keep thinking a showgirl was nothing more than a cheerleader with feathers in her hair. Zach stopped himself from bringing up the showgirl, however. Jenny didn't seem to approve of showgirls. Instead Zach decided he'd list his good points.

"I might not be as well mannered as their father…and educated," Zach continued. She could stop him at any time, but she didn't seem inclined to do so. "And I'm sure they still miss him something fierce. But, one thing I can guarantee, and that is you can trust your kids with me."

Jenny was speechless. Zach wanted to spend time with her children.

"They're not perfect children." Jenny felt she should let him know. "Lisa bites her nails."

Zach nodded. "I noticed. But I think maybe she'll grow out of it. It's not something to worry about, is it?"

"I asked Mrs. Hargrove about it. She said maybe it's just the move."

Zach nodded. "I'm sure moving around is hard on kids."

Moving around is hard on everyone, Jenny thought, but didn't say it. She'd finally decided that God wanted her and the children in Dry Creek, but that didn't mean that sometimes she didn't wonder what it would have been like if she'd dug in her heels and refused to leave El Monte. At least there she would never have been stranded miles away from the nearest neighbor with a man who cared about whether or not Lisa bit her nails.

"Mommy!" The call came from the kitchen.

"Oh, the pancakes," Jenny said. "I better get going."

"Take your time," Zach said as he turned toward where he'd laid his coat. "I need to get those pipes put back together before you can cook anything, anyway."

"Oh, I forgot."

"Now that it's light, it'll only take a few minutes." Zach walked out of the living room and into the kitchen.

Jenny stood up. "In that case, I'll dress first."

"Wear something warm," Zach called back from the kitchen. "We need to get that tree in before it starts to snow again. I told Lisa I think I know where we'll find one."

Jenny nodded. How was she supposed to protect her children's hearts from this man when he promised them a Christmas tree in the middle of a Montana blizzard?

The pancakes fried up nice and brown and Jenny was even able to warm the maple syrup. Everyone ate their fill, and they had barely pushed their chairs back from the table before Lisa asked if it was time to go to get the tree.

"I don't see why not," Zach said. He didn't like the looks of the heavy gray clouds outside.

"There's the dishes," Jenny reminded everyone.

Lisa and Andy groaned.

"It's going to snow later," Zach said. "Maybe we should go right away."

Lisa and Andy looked at Zach and beamed.

"Well, maybe just this once we can do the dishes after we get back," Jenny conceded.

"You can put them to soak," Andy offered. Soaking the dishes was Andy's favorite way to cope with them. Lisa, on the other hand, carefully scrubbed each dish with a sponge.

"I'll at least clear the table while everyone gets dressed," Jenny said to her children. "And remember double socks today."

Jenny had put on panty hose under her jeans and two flannel shirts over a T-shirt. She figured that should keep her warm enough outside. She figured wrong.

"Don't you have anything warmer than those shirts?" Zach asked when the children had left the kitchen.

It wasn't until this morning that Zach had figured out that the men's flannel shirts Jenny was wearing had to be left from her husband's wardrobe. No wonder the woman wouldn't let them go. If they'd been real flannel, they'd probably keep her comfortable in the cold. But they were the thin, city flannel that was meant for style instead of weather.

"What's wrong with these shirts?"

"Nothing. They're just not warm enough."

Jenny lifted her chin. "They'll have to do."

"You could borrow a sweatshirt from me," Zach offered and then held his breath. "I've got a new one—not even worn—picked it up at a rodeo in Fargo a couple of weeks ago."

"What makes you think it's warmer than my shirts?"

"Those are California shirts. Made for the

beach. The sweatshirt was made for North Dakota wear."

"I wouldn't want to impose."

"And I wouldn't want you to catch your death of cold." Zach thought he had the upper hand, but he decided to cinch it. "Who will take care of your kids if you come down with pneumonia?"

"I won't get sick," Jenny assured him. She couldn't afford to get sick.

"Then you'll wear the sweatshirt," Zach ordered. "And the sheepskin coat."

"Oh, I can't possibly—I can't wear your coat," Jenny sputtered. She needed to draw the line somewhere. She was used to taking care of herself. It wouldn't be good to let down her guard and become used to someone doing things for her. She'd have to cope on her own again when he was gone. Besides, she'd always been a fair person. "You will get just as cold as me. It's your coat. You'll need it."

"I can't wear it, anyway, while I chop down the tree." Zach only hoped they found a tree to chop down. He'd look foolish chopping down a thistle bush. "You might as well wear it. If not, it'll just stay sitting on the seat behind me."

Jenny looked at the coat. Maybe she could let her guard down a little. It was Christmas, after all. And the coat was lined with a heavy knotted wool. "That's not real sheepskin, is it?"

Zach grinned. "Imitation."

Jenny walked over and touched the coat. The rough, knobby lining was warm.

"Try it on."

Zach held the sleeves to the coat as Jenny slipped her arms into it.

"Feels like fur," Jenny said. The coat made her feel warm for the first time in days. She almost felt like purring.

"Now you're ready to go." Zach looked at Jenny with satisfaction. She finally looked like a Montana woman.

Lisa was the first one to spot the trees. After Zach had scraped the ice off the front and side windows, the four of them had squeezed into the postal truck and driven down the road that ran along the fence of the Collins property. Just like Zach remembered from the previous day, the only trees around were at the bottom of the coulee about a half mile past the fence, just as the road turned up the hill to go to the house.

Zach had to give Lisa credit. She had leaned over her mother's shoulder so she could look out the side window. Since Lisa had already insisted

Jenny roll down the window on their side, that meant Lisa's nose was cold enough to be red.

"I see one. I see one. I see one. Stop right here." Lisa bounced on her feet as she stood on the floor of the postal truck and half leaned out the passenger-side window.

"We need to pick one that doesn't have any pine cones," Jenny announced as she pulled out a narrow, green book from a bag she carried. She started to flip through the pages. "And it's also good to find one that's at least—" she turned a page "—eight, maybe even nine feet tall."

Lisa seemed familiar with her mother's green book. The girl didn't even look at the book, she just nodded dutifully. "We will, Mama."

"What's that?" Zach eyed the book that Jenny read. He had assumed the bag held cookies or crackers in case the kids got hungry.

"It's my *Montana Guidebook*. It's got a chapter on caring for local trees." Jenny lifted her chin. Mrs. Hargrove had given her the book when Jenny said she wanted to learn more about the area. "I don't know very much about Montana. But the people who wrote this book do. They say there's no excuse for just stripping the land of its trees. A good farmer doesn't do that."

"We're only talking one tree," Zach reminded her as he turned off the ignition. He'd already pulled the truck to the side of the road in an area between two snowdrifts. "That's hardly stripping your land."

Jenny tightened her grip on the green book. "The trees with pine cones are needed to make seeds for new tall trees."

"Well, there is that." Zach nodded.

He didn't have the heart to tell her that it would take more than a few pine cones to make nine-foot pine trees grow on her land. The trees at the bottom of the coulee were hunched over from the wind. He doubted any of them would ever grow more than five feet tall. And those were the lucky ones. Any tree seed unfortunate enough to fall on the top sides of the coulee would never live to grow even to four feet. The wind would see to that.

"I want a tree with an angel hook," Lisa announced as she sat back down on the floor in the back of the postal truck and pulled on her mittens.

"That's just something they put on trees at the lot where we got them in L.A., dear," Jenny said as she sat her book down on the tray that ran along the front of the cab. "These trees won't have them."

"Will they have one of those kissie-toe

things?" Andy asked as he crawled up front and held out a mittenless hand to his mother.

"You mean mistletoe?" Jenny asked hesitantly. She had hoped Andy had forgotten about the kiss he'd seen last night. She put her hand in the pocket of Andy's coat and pulled out his missing mitten. "No, the tree won't have that."

"Then how is Mr. Lightning going to learn how to kiss?" Andy forgot about his mitten and just stood in the space between Jenny and Zach.

Zach felt a little hand clamp on to his arm and he looked over to the boy. Andy's eyes were earnest with worry as they looked back at him. Zach would have joked with the boy, but he looked over the little one's head and saw Jenny. Joking might not be the best idea, Zach decided.

"Mr. Lightning doesn't need to learn how to kiss," Jenny finally said firmly as she reached around the truck's gearshift to capture Andy's bare hand. Jenny pulled the mitten on Andy's hand. "Now, be sure you have your coats buttoned up tight before you go outside."

Zach held back his grin until his muscles ached. He could watch Jenny's face blush a hundred times and never grow tired of the wonder of it.

"I'm zipped," Andy said happily as he wiggled back into the back of the truck.

"Me, too," Lisa said as she unhooked the back door.

"Wait at the edge of the coulee. We'll all walk down together," Jenny called as the two children scrambled out. "I need to talk to Mr. Lucas for a minute first."

Jenny wished she didn't blush. "I'm sorry. Sometimes kids say the craziest things."

"I suppose it's because of Christmas." Zach agreed solemnly. It occurred to him that he hadn't been able to get a clear picture of Jenny's eyes last night when they had kissed. The candlelight hadn't given off enough light. "I hear everyone's crazy at Christmas."

"Yes, yes, that must be it." Jenny was relieved he seemed to understand. "They just get excited, and…well, they don't mean anything by it."

"I must say, though, it is a little troubling." Zach turned so that he was looking squarely at Jenny.

"What is?" Jenny turned to face Zach.

Zach reached up to touch Jenny's cheek. It was cool and smooth as silk. "How can I let your son think I don't know how to kiss his mother?"

"He's talking about air kisses," Jenny whispered. She felt the man's thumb as he rubbed it down her cheek. Her cheek was cold, and his thumb felt like a hot brand, marking her cheek as his own. "The kind you blow across the room."

"Seems an awfully risky way to send a kiss," Zach said softly as he moved closer. "And not nearly as satisfying."

Jenny swallowed. Or at least she tried to—she was having a hard time even breathing. "We need to go get the tree."

Zach must have kissed more than a thousand women. Never once in all those times had he wanted a signal as desperately as he wanted one from Jenny. He didn't want to kiss her unless he knew she wanted him to kiss her.

"Is that what you want?" There, he thought to himself, he'd just put the question out there. He didn't want to have any doubts. "The kids are warm. They can wait a minute."

"No, I don't want to... Yes, I mean...the kids—" Jenny stumbled. She needed to remember the kids. She was going to find a steady, churchgoing man to be a father to her kids. She couldn't afford to be sweet-talked by a cowboy who was just passing through. Besides. "The kids want a tree."

Zach swallowed. Never let it be said he took rejection badly. He was a grown man. He knew the odds. He put his hand on the door handle of the truck and pushed. "Well then, let's go get us a tree."

Before they got to the trees, they all came to a slight indentation in the ground.

"Mrs. Hargrove told me that's where the first house in this area sat," Jenny said. "One of her husband's ancestors settled here by the creek."

Zach walked over to the place. There was a raised edge to the indentation that showed the outline of what must have been the house. Zach guessed the house had been half sod and half stone. It certainly hadn't been very large.

"His name was Jake Hargrove. He'd taken in some children and wanted to live away from the fort," Jenny continued from where she stood. "The kids were part Dakota. Both girls."

"Girls like me?" Lisa asked as she followed Zach over to the ruin and stood where the house would have been. "My age, I mean?"

"We'll have to ask Mrs. Hargrove how old they were," Jenny said.

"I wonder if they went out to get a Christmas tree," Lisa said. "Like we're doing."

"I don't know," Jenny said.

"If they did, they were probably quick about it," Zach added as he looked up to the sky. The clouds were turning dark.

"We'll be fast," Lisa said as she left the old

house and ran toward where the trees were. "I see one already."

The tree was deformed. But Lisa had happily pointed out the one she wanted, and Zach had dutifully cut it, and they had all dragged it up out of the coulee.

"It's got a place for stars," Lisa said as she patted one of the branches.

When they got back to the house, they set the tree up in the middle of the living room. Jenny produced a plastic bucket, and they poured rocks around the tree trunk to make it stay upright. Even with the extra height of the bucket, however, the tree didn't top four feet. It also had a tendency to tilt to the left.

"It's beautiful," Jenny declared loyally when they were finished.

"It's crooked," Lisa confessed, a worried frown on her face.

"Some of the most beautiful things in the world are crooked." Zach anchored the tree deeper into the bucket of rocks. "Remember that leaning tower in Italy."

"Yeah." Lisa smiled. "We'll just have an Italian tree."

Jenny had taken Mrs. Hargrove's camera with them and she'd taken a picture of Lisa, Andy and Zach as they all measured that tree down at the bottom of the coulee. And then she'd taken a couple more of them dragging the tree up out of the coulee. "And I'm sure we'll think of something for decorations."

"We don't have decorations?" Lisa stopped studying the tree and turned to her mother. It was clear that any worry about the tilting of the tree was forgotten. "We have to have decorations."

"We can make decorations," Jenny said firmly. She should have shown her children how to make decorations in the years past. It's just that Stephen never liked the mess that projects like that made and so it was easier to just buy things at the thrift stores.

"But how can we make stars?" Lisa said worriedly. "Stars need to sparkle."

Zach sat down on the sofa to get a better look at the tree. He didn't know whether he was coming or going. He'd looked ahead down the road on the way back from getting the tree just to see if he could make it into Dry Creek. He could tell it would be foolish to leave this house, especially because the clouds had started to grow even more gray.

Of course, no matter how foolish it would be to leave, staying might be worse.

Life had really pulled a fast one on him. Here

he was, snowed in with a family that was everything like the family on that Christmas card he'd seen when he was ten. Everyone cared about each other. They even cared about the stray cat out in the barn. And they didn't need a tree to be happy together, but they had a tree, anyway. They made a perfect Christmas card picture. Sure, the father might be missing from the picture, but the man used to be in the picture. For years and years, this Stephen guy had been the husband and father in this family.

The man was dead and buried. And Zach still envied him like he'd never envied anyone in his life. That man had had it all.

"I bet he never rode a horse, though," Zach said aloud to himself.

"Huh?" Jenny looked over at Zach. For the first time today, he looked a little frayed around the edges. Zach was sitting on the sofa with his shoulders hunched forward and his hands clutching an empty cup that had held coffee.

"Horse." Andy caught the one word that interested him. He had been sitting on the floor at Zach's feet. Now he jumped up and stood at Zach's knee. "Are we going to ride a horse? Huh? Are we?"

"We don't have a horse," Jenny answered her son.

"And lights," Lisa moaned. She was still looking at the tree. "We don't have any lights."

"I can take the lights off those reindeer horns on the postal truck," Zach offered as he stood up. He might not be part of this family, but he still wanted this Christmas to be perfect, Christmas tree and all. "They are on some kind of batteries."

Lisa brightened. "That's right."

"And we can make stars out of aluminum foil." Jenny started toward the kitchen. "And I have some red yarn for bows."

"Mr. Lightning has a horse," Andy said softly as he watched Zach walk toward the kitchen door.

"That horse is sick," Lisa said in disgust. "You can't ride a sick horse."

Zach stopped himself from promising the boy a ride. It would be a promise he might not be able to keep. Once Thunder was well, they needed to keep driving down to Vegas. He and Thunder were both roving souls. And it wasn't as if Jenny would ever invite him back for a visit. "I'll bring in the reindeer horns. Maybe we can rig you up a horse to ride from them."

"See," Andy said to his sister. "I am going to get to ride."

"That's just a pretend horse."

"I still get to ride it."

Lisa just shook her head. "First you have to help make stars."

Zach stepped into the kitchen. Jenny had opened a drawer on the counter and was pulling out slender tubes. "I know I had tinfoil here somewhere."

"I have some foil in the truck."

Jenny looked up, relieved. "You do?"

"Wrapped around half a dozen plates of cookies."

"I could replace the foil with waxed paper," Jenny offered. "That way your cookies won't dry out."

"I thought I'd bring them in, anyway. The kids will like them."

"Oh, we couldn't take your cookies."

"They're not my cookies. They were meant for Mrs. Brown or Charley. They'd want the kids to have them."

Why was it, Zach asked himself, that it was so difficult to give that woman anything? Even a porcupine had fewer prickles.

"Well, thank you." Jenny pushed the empty tube of foil back into the drawer. Why was it that the man insisted on being so nice? Couldn't he see that she was determined not to let him get under her skin? "I'll pay you for them, of course."

Zach just looked at her as he grabbed his coat off the hook. What was it with this woman? "I can't sell you a plate of Christmas cookies. Besides, I don't need your money."

Jenny was going to point out that everyone needed money, but the man was out of the door before she could. Still, she had made her point. She wanted to keep things on a businesslike level between them. Money helped do that. She didn't like accepting things from him. It made her feel as if they were friends.

No, she admitted to herself, it didn't make her feel as if they were friends. Friends stayed around. They didn't leave and take your heart with them. No, the last thing Zach offered was friendship. At the moment he was a stranger, just passing through, and she would do well to remember it.

She'd do better to bond with that poor cat out in the barn. At least the cat would be around long enough to get her kittens born and settled. Jenny supposed she'd need to find a way to coax the cat into the laundry room before Zach left. They couldn't leave kittens out in the barn without heat, and there would be no one to tend the fire at night once the cowboy left.

## Chapter Eight

Zach had a towel wrapped around his fingers and a hot sheet of metal in his hand. It wasn't the best time to be watching Jenny as she watched the sky. He wondered if she knew her blond curls shone with golden highlights as she stood in the thin light that came through the window above the kitchen sink. And the long curve of her neck as she looked up—well, as Zach already knew, it wasn't the best of times for him to be holding a hot sheet of metal.

He'd already burned himself once today when Jenny bent over to pick up a spoon that fell on the floor. Of course, it had almost been worth it when Jenny insisted on rubbing some kind of an ointment on his thumb. She'd been shy about touching him, and Zach had found it more exciting than any flirtation he'd ever encountered.

"Expecting geese?" Zach carefully set the cookie sheet on the pot holders Jenny had laid out on the counter. The kitchen was warm and the sounds of the children in the living room made him feel a contentment he'd never known. For one brief day he was inside the Christmas picture.

Andy had gone into the living room to fold tinfoil stars with Lisa. Jenny had been doing dishes, until she stopped to look up at the sky.

Jenny turned toward him. "It's below zero out there. There're no geese."

Zach nodded. "I know, but the way you've been watching that sky I figured you must be watching for something."

"I was looking at the clouds." Jenny had resisted the temptation to bring her green *Montana Guidebook* out from her bedroom. Before starting the dishes, she'd carefully read the different cloud descriptions. If she could just match the clouds outside with the right picture in her guidebook, she should be able to tell if it would snow more today. Unless there was more snow, Zach might leave. She didn't want that to happen—for Andy's sake, she told herself. Gray and heavy clouds meant snow. The clouds outside were gray, but she wasn't sure if they were heavy enough.

"Ah." Zach started lifting the cookies off the pan and onto a platter.

"What makes air heavy?"

Jenny hardly recognized the cowboy. He had flour on his face and a sprinkling of cinnamon on his shirt. He'd tied an old dish towel around his waist. If the cereal people could only see him now, they'd take a whole new set of pictures for the backs of their boxes.

"Moisture, I guess." Zach carefully nudged the angel cookies to the left of the platter so there would be room for a few sugar-cookie trees. He'd never thought he would ever be baking Christmas cookies. "Don't tell me you're worried, too. I thought Andy was the only one."

"Andy's worried?" Jenny didn't like that her son was worried about whether or not it would snow. Of course, Zach had probably mentioned the roads to Andy. "Have you said something to make him worry you'd leave?"

"Me? No. He's not worried about me. He's worried about Santa Claus. Andy's afraid that if it rains instead of snows Santa won't be able to land his sled on the roof because it'll be too slippery." Zach kept his tone light. "It seems he remembers when you tried to fix the roof."

"Oh."

"Something about the roof being slippery

because it was raining." Zach took a deep breath so his panic wouldn't show. He knew it was none of his business what this woman had decided to do a few weeks ago. But what if she had fallen off the roof instead of just sliding down the roof a bit? He wouldn't have even been there to get her to the doctor. "I guess that guidebook of yours didn't tell you that you shouldn't be climbing around on a roof in the rain. Especially not a pitched roof like this one. It's dangerous."

"Well, I didn't know the roof leaked until it started to rain for the second time."

"That's what buckets are for." Zach put the empty cookie sheet back on top of the stove. He had one more tray in the oven. "You wait until the roof is dry to work on it. Besides, you shouldn't be fixing your own roof, anyway." Zach bent his head down to open the oven and mumbled the rest. "I'll see it gets done for you."

Jenny didn't think she had heard him right. "But you can't do it, either. Snow's no better than rain. Well, it has to be worse—snow is wet and ice both at the same time. Besides…" Jenny didn't finish. They both knew he would be gone before the snow melted.

Zach swallowed. The hot air from inside the

oven felt good on his face. He reached in for the tray of snowman cookies. He might as well say this while he was facing the oven. He didn't expect Jenny would like it. But he had given it some thought. "I've decided—when I go back to Dry Creek—I'm going to give Charley money to hire someone to put a new roof on this house."

Jenny gasped. She forgot all about the dishrag in her hand. "But, you can't. Why, that's way too much…you can't possibly."

Zach pulled the tray of cookies out of the oven and straightened up. "Consider it a Christmas present."

Jenny dropped the dishrag back into the dish water. "That's not a Christmas present—a Christmas present is socks or a pin—something small. A roof is way bigger than a Christmas present." The warm air from the oven floated across the kitchen toward her. "Besides, you don't even like Christmas."

"Maybe not, but I like solid roofs."

"But you can't pay to have a new roof put on my house. Why, what would Charley and Mrs. Hargrove think?"

"They'd think you were getting a new roof."

No, Jenny thought to herself, they'd think she was getting a new husband. Which was ridiculous, of course. Anyone could see the cowboy wasn't the kind of guy to marry anyone. He would never settle down. He'd just—no, Jenny realized with a start, Charley and Mrs. Hargrove wouldn't think of marriage at all.

She'd been out of the dating game for so long, she didn't recognize the obvious. Maybe Charley and Mrs. Hargrove wouldn't think it, but other people would think the cowboy was doing her favors because she'd been generous to him in the way of women throughout time. A lot of people would think that. "I could never accept a gift that expensive. It'd be hundreds of dollars."

Try thousands, Zach thought. But he wouldn't sleep well nights thinking Jenny might be crawling around up on that roof. And paying someone to do it was the only way. Unless… "If you won't let me pay someone, I'll come back and put a new roof up myself."

Jenny looked at him as if he'd offered to burn her house down instead of seeing that it stayed dry. "I have the children to think of, you know. Not to mention the fact that I have to live in this community." Jenny paused. "I'm afraid you wouldn't get anything in exchange for the roof."

"I wouldn't—" Zach had been scooping the

cookies off the sheet and turned too fast. The back of his hand hit the hot sheet. He barely felt the burn. He'd figured out what Jenny was saying, and he didn't like it. Not that he wouldn't have tried to find an angle with any other woman he found attractive. "I can think of the children, too, you know. And I wasn't expecting anything in return for the roof."

Jenny had noticed his wince when his hand hit the sheet. She reached in her pocket for the tube of ointment. "Then why were you offering it?" She held out her hand. "Here, let me see your hand."

Zach held out his closed fist. The ointment felt cool until Jenny rubbed it around on the back of his hand. Then his whole body heated up. "Can't someone do something nice for you just because—" Zach scrambled for a reason "—just because it's Christmas?"

"You're doing it because of Christmas? You?" Jenny obviously wasn't convinced.

Sometimes, Zach decided, a man needed to stay with the cards he'd been dealt, even if they were losing cards. "I have a lot of Christmas presents to make up for. From the past."

"I didn't know you in the past." Jenny held Zach's burned hand while she reached over to the counter and picked up the roll of gauze she'd used on Zach's thumb earlier. She started to unroll the gauze. "You don't owe me any presents."

Zach closed his eyes. Why did she have to make it so hard? "Maybe I've decided it would be too difficult to track down everyone I've known over the years and give them a belated present."

Jenny wrapped gauze around Zach's hand. "So this roof—it's like penance for all your past missed gifts."

"Something like that." Zach closed his eyes wearily. He hoped she never discovered that just because he didn't believe in Christmas didn't mean he'd been stingy in the past. Ever since Zach had started making good money on the rodeo circuit, he'd given some very nice presents to people. Of course, they were usually checks. Some of them had even been for dollar amounts that would be more than Jenny's roof would take. Never, however, had Zach had as much trouble with anyone accepting a present as he was having with Jenny.

"And you're not expecting to sleep with me in return?" Jenny asked the question crisply. She was just making sure they understood each other.

Zach opened his eyes at that. "Lady, you'll

barely kiss me. I'm not fool enough to think a roof would get us to where you're thinking."

Zach hoped she'd protest. Hoped she'd say it might at least get him a date. She didn't.

Instead Jenny slowly knotted the gauze on his hand. She didn't even raise her eyes to his but kept them on his burn. "But I don't have anything nearly that expensive to give you in return."

Zach smiled. So it was her pride that was bothering her. He turned his bandaged hand so that he held hers. "At the rate I'm going, maybe you should just give me that ointment in your pocket and a roll of that gauze. We'll figure you've saved me from a life of disfiguring burns."

Jenny looked up and smiled back, but she didn't remove her hand. "Cookie baking can be dangerous."

"I never knew kitchen duty could be so hazardous." Zach couldn't control his thumb as it rubbed the back of Jenny's hand. Jenny had been washing dishes and her hands were still slightly damp from the water. Even damp, Zach wagered they were smoother than other women's hands. Of course, maybe he was just partial to them.

Jenny's cheeks were pink as she smiled. "If you think this is exciting, wait until tomorrow. You can help me with the ham. And—if you really want a thrill—you can help open the can of yams I'm going to bake."

"It can't be any harder than baking these cookies." Zach settled back into holding Jenny's hand.

Zach couldn't remember ever holding a woman's hand before. He couldn't remember *wanting* to hold a woman's hand. He was always too intent on winning a bigger prize. What a fool he'd been, he thought as he squeezed Jenny's hand. He hadn't known what he was missing. He would remember this moment forever.

The warm smell of sugar cookies made the kitchen cozy. Jenny had rolled the dough thin, and Lisa and Andy had used cookie cutters to shape snowmen, angels, bells and trees. Zach had measured the ingredients and helped Andy stir. Everyone had sprinkled colored sugar on the different shapes before Zach slipped the cookie sheets into the oven.

The sky outside was gray, and only a thin light shone through the windows. The electricity was still off but Jenny had lit a candle and set it on the folding table. The glow of the candle cast yellow light all around the kitchen.

Jenny held her breath. She couldn't remember ever having someone sit with her at the end of a day and hold her hand. It should feel innocent, even with the hypnotic feel of Zach's thumb as it traced circles on the back of her hand. But it didn't feel the least bit innocent. It was one of the most intense moments she'd ever experienced. Too bad intense was a mistake.

"Thanks for helping with everything," Jenny finally said to Zach as she gently removed her hand. "You got the tree. You took the kids out to see the cat."

"Of course, we didn't find her," Zach added. They had heard the cat hiss when they entered the barn, but they couldn't find her back amid the hay bales.

"Still, you're making it a wonderful Christmas."

Jenny looked around her kitchen with satisfaction. For the first time, she didn't notice all the things she didn't have. Instead she saw that the folding table still had scraps of tinfoil from the star shapes that Lisa had cut earlier and the kitchen counter was covered with every platter she owned. Each platter was covered with Christmas sugar cookies. Such a wonderful Christmas merited a wonderful present for the man who had helped make it all possible.

"I can think of a better gift for you than a

first-aid kit," Jenny said firmly. She was full of goodwill. Everyone inside her home would have a good Christmas if it was in her power to give them one.

The light coming in from the kitchen window cast shadows around Zach's eyes. "I'm not expecting anything. You don't need to—I mean, the roof doesn't require a present. It's just because—"

"No, I need a present for you." Jenny closed her eyes. How could a cowboy in worn jeans and a towel apron covered with cookie dough look so handsome? Well, it wasn't his fault she couldn't keep her eyes off him. He'd been good to her children, and she owed him a Christmas present. She did a mental review of the boxes in her bedroom. "Maybe something of Stephen's—"

"No." The word sounded abrupt even to Zach's ears. Jenny's eyes flew open. To hide his confusion, Zach turned and stole a warm cookie from a platter. "I mean, you should save his things for Andy and Lisa. When they're older, they'll want some things to remember him by."

Jenny wondered if her children would remember their father in twenty years. If they did, it wouldn't be because of some sweater or tie.

"He must have been a wonderful father and husband." Zach tried to sound casual as he took a bite out of the cookie.

Zach hated himself for trying to find out more about the man, but the man's very existence bothered him like a scab that wasn't healing right. Maybe someone would let something slip, and Zach could learn the secret that this Stephen had known about being part of a family like this one.

Maybe—Zach didn't dare even hope—but maybe the secret was something Zach could learn if he only had a few pointers. Zach almost choked on the rest of what he had to say, but he said it, anyway. "I wish I could have known him. What was he like?"

"Like?" Jenny's voice squeaked. She never talked about Stephen. He was not only a closed chapter in her life, she'd buried the book, as well.

"Yeah. Did he have any hobbies?" Zach supposed the man liked opera. Women always seemed to like opera. Zach preferred a guitar player in a bar anytime. Still, he supposed he could learn to endure opera. "Anything you and he did for special evenings?"

Jenny tried hard to think. She and Stephen hadn't done anything social even in the years before he was sick. Stephen preferred to go out with his male friends rather than stay home with her, and he never wanted to spend the money for a babysitter so they could go out together. "We didn't have a lot of money."

"I see." Zach figured that meant they spent a lot of cozy evenings at home putting together jigsaw puzzles and watching videos. The very thought of it depressed him. Zach would have had a better chance of competing if Jenny had mentioned dinners in fancy restaurants and dancing. He could afford to fly her to Paris for a weekend. It was the home things he wasn't sure he'd ever get right.

The outside light was fading in the kitchen, and the shine of the candle on the table was growing more golden. Zach's face picked up the glow of the candle. He was concentrating on the cookie in his hand with an intensity that reminded Jenny of his picture on the back of that cereal box.

It was the cereal-box picture that gave Jenny the courage to decide to tell Zach the truth about Stephen. She wanted to tell someone. She really did. The words always just seemed to stick in her throat. But if she pretended she was still only talking to the back of that box, maybe she could get the words out.

"Stephen—" Jenny began and swallowed.

She felt almost relieved now that she had decided to tell someone. Even if that someone was just a cowboy who was on the back of a cereal box. "Stephen was, well, it wasn't so much what he was, it's what he— Well, you know I've told you that he wasn't—" Jenny stopped. Zach had turned and was looking at her. All of a sudden, he didn't look anything like his picture on the cereal box.

"Yeah," Zach prompted her.

"I, ah…" Jenny knew it was her chance. She also knew she was a coward. She didn't know what Zach would think of her if she told him about Stephen. Lots of men thought any marital unhappiness was the wife's fault. Maybe Zach would think that, too. "I…we got married awfully young."

Zach almost groaned. No wonder Jenny didn't want to kiss another man. Stephen was probably the only man she'd ever even dated. "You must have been very much in love."

"Uh…" Jenny swallowed. She would try again.

Jenny never got a chance. The quiet giggles from the living room had grown louder and finally they were at the kitchen door.

"Mama, come look," Lisa called as she stood in the doorway.

The house was in shadows.

"Oh, I better get the lantern lit," Jenny said. She'd talk to Zach later. It wasn't that she wouldn't have talked to him, she assured herself. It just wasn't the time yet. She'd tell him all about Stephen. And soon. Just not right this minute. She couldn't risk the children hearing about Stephen.

"Mr. Lightning," Andy called from the living room. "Come see the stars."

Zach followed Jenny into the living room, and the light from the lantern she was carrying made the tinfoil stars reflect a thousand lights. The tree glowed with the reflections. Zach had unwrapped the Christmas lights from around the reindeer horns that had hung on the postal-truck hood. He'd then clipped the lights to the branches of the Christmas tree. The battery for the lights was nestled on top of the rocks at the bottom of the tree. So far, no one had turned on the lights.

"They're lovely," Jenny said as she put one hand on Lisa's shoulder and smiled at Andy. "I've never seen so many stars."

"Can we turn the lights on now?" Lisa asked. "It's almost dark."

Jenny had told the children earlier that they would turn on the tree lights when it grew dark. Jenny wasn't sure how much power the batteries had left, and she didn't want to run the batteries dry before it even grew dark.

"Let's have some soup first." Jenny looked at her watch. How had the day gone so fast? "It's almost five o'clock. Then we can read the Christmas story before you go off to bed."

"But that will still be too early," Lisa protested. "I wanted to wrap your present."

Zach had hidden the jewelry box the kids had made for their mother earlier this morning. The jewelry box had really been a small wooden toolbox that Zach had kept his leather-working tools inside. Andy had glued some beach shells he'd found in California on top of the box and Lisa had glued a piece of velvet on the inside of the box.

Wrapping presents, Jenny thought in dismay. "But I don't have any paper. Oh, I knew I wasn't ready for Christmas."

"Wrapping paper isn't necessary," Zach said, hoping he was right. He was wrong.

"Yes, it is," Lisa said, and she looked up at Zach as if he was a magician with a hat that still had a few rabbits left inside of it.

"I don't have any—oh, wait." Zach remembered. "I do have paper. In the postal truck. Mrs. Brown carries around a tube of brown postal paper. And tape."

"Brown paper?" Lisa looked skeptical.

"I think there might be some red stamps and some markers." Zach wasn't sure what all Mrs. Brown kept in the postal bin that ran along the right-top side of the truck.

"We can make Christmas paper," Jenny said in relief. The kids would remember Christmas paper they had made themselves a lot longer than anything she could buy.

"Just remember, you need to go to bed early tonight," Jenny said firmly. "Remember what we said? If you go to bed early, you can get up early tomorrow morning."

And, if they go to bed early, Jenny added to herself, she and Zach would have time to make the presents for the children they'd talked about earlier. Zach had told her his ideas, and she knew the children would love the gifts he had suggested.

"All right," Lisa agreed reluctantly.

"Can I have cereal instead of soup for supper?" Andy asked.

Andy had also asked to have Ranger Flakes for lunch when the rest of them had eaten tuna sandwiches. Jenny had given in then. "You've got to eat more than cereal."

"I can have a cookie, too," Andy offered.

Jenny appealed to Zach. "You talk to him."

Zach smiled. He was glad the cereal executives couldn't hear him now. "Real cowboys don't eat cereal for every meal. They need other things, too, to stay healthy. Maybe you should try some soup tonight."

"Are you eating soup?" Andy asked as he walked over and wrapped his arms around Zach's leg.

"I sure am."

"Okay," Andy agreed. "I'll have soup. And crackers?"

"Yeah, we have crackers. And peaches for dessert." Jenny tried to remember everything she had in the cupboards. She was grateful Stephen's uncle had had the good sense to see that the kitchen stove operated off the propane tank like the furnace did. With the electricity still out, they wouldn't be eating anything warm if he hadn't.

Zach left his hand resting on Andy's head. Zach liked the solid weight of the boy as Andy leaned against his leg. "Let's go set the table for your mom."

"I know where the bowls are," Lisa announced as she led the way.

Supper was by candlelight, and Zach was content. He'd eaten candlelight dinners in five-star restaurants at the top of skyscrapers and on cruise ships. At none of those dinners had the conversation lagged or the soup been cold. But he didn't even have to debate the issue. He wouldn't trade this candlelight meal for any one of the others.

"At least the peaches should be all right," Jenny said quietly.

"It was a wonderful meal," Zach assured her. "Wholesome."

"I could heat up some more tomato soup, now that the stove has cooled down." Jenny hadn't realized that using the oven of the stove all afternoon would affect the burners. It meant they wouldn't stay lit for very long.

"I'm content."

Jenny wondered if she should admit to Zach that she was content, too. She wondered at the ease she felt around him. Earlier in the day Jenny had realized she was relaxing around Zach because he didn't criticize her the way she had expected any man would. Zach seemed to be pleased with whatever she had to offer in the way of meals and household comforts.

Zach was a big change from her late husband. Stephen had been visibly unhappy if the laundry wasn't ironed right or the meals weren't to his liking. No wonder she'd been tired all those years when she'd been married,

Jenny thought to herself in amazement. She'd been trying to make things perfect for Stephen. And perfection had been hard to maintain when she had two small children to care for as well.

Of course, Jenny told herself, it was easy for Zach to accept things the way they were. He wouldn't be around long and he probably just didn't care.

"I do know how to cook a good meal," she added in self-defense. "It's just the stove and all. I'm learning."

"We're all learning." Zach pushed his chair away from the table. "Let me get the peaches for you."

"After peaches, I want to make wrapping paper," Lisa said.

Jenny rinsed the dishes from supper and left them in the sink. Amazing how liberating that felt. For the second time today she hadn't needed to rush to do the dishes as if she had something to prove to someone. Instead the four of them sat at the folding table and made wrapping paper.

Andy liked to stamp. He'd stamped a red *FRAGILE* over a length of brown postal paper. The stamp was upside down in some places and sideways in others. Jenny noticed that the confused jumble of it all did manage to look festive.

Lisa was drawing bells with a red pen on another length of brown postal paper.

"I'll need to remember to pay Mrs. Brown for all this," Jenny said.

"I bet she'd like a picture, too," Zach said as he stood up and walked to the kitchen counter. The woman deserved to see them as they concentrated on decorating the postal paper. "You should take one for Mrs. Hargrove and Charley, too."

"Great idea," Jenny said as she accepted the camera Zach handed to her.

Jenny snapped four pictures and pulled them out to dry. She'd taken a dozen or so pictures of the children over the day. There was one of Andy and Zach cutting out cookies. There was one of Lisa and Zach stringing the lights on the Christmas tree.

Each picture Jenny took, she took an extra. One of the shots was for herself. The other one was for a Christmas present for Zach. She'd thought about going through the box of Stephen's ties and sweaters, but even though Zach wouldn't be wearing either one around Jenny, she didn't like to picture him in anything but the clothes he already had. She didn't want to look at the cowboy and see any reminders of Stephen.

Actually, she thought she might take the whole

box of Stephen's things and tie it up tight with some postal string before setting it at the back of the large closet in her bedroom. Zach was right. Andy and Lisa might want to see the things someday, but for now, Jenny wanted it tucked away where she didn't have to see it every day.

Jenny couldn't help but wonder, as she listened to her children giggle while they talked with Zach, what her life would have been like if she had married a man like Zach instead of one like Stephen.

Well—she shook herself—that was a pointless thing to wonder about, and on a Christmas Eve.

## Chapter Nine

Zach had never heard the Christmas story read to children. Oh, he knew the story—sort of, anyway. The star. The wise men. The shepherds. The angels. The baby in the manger. But he'd never seen it through the eyes of children.

Zach sat backward on a folding chair with his arms resting on the back. He loved watching Jenny as she sat on the sofa with one child on either side of her and read them the Christmas story. The three of them believed that story had really happened. Zach could tell just by watching them, and he envied them. He wished he knew God well enough to trust him like that.

"And that's why we have hope today," Jenny said as she closed the children's book. "Because a long time ago on Christmas Eve, the baby Jesus was born in a manger in Bethlehem."

"I wish He could have been born in our barn," Andy said.

"Like our kittens are going to be born tonight," Lisa added hopefully.

"Well, maybe somewhat like the kittens," Jenny said with a smile.

"We need to take the mama cat some warm milk," Lisa said as she looked up at Zach. "She'll be hungry."

"All we have left is dry milk," Jenny said.

"That will do," Zach said. "Maybe with some crackers in it."

Jenny had moved the lantern into the living room, and it was hanging from a hook she'd rigged up from the ceiling fan. The lantern gave off a yellowish light that bathed the room in a warm glow. The smell of recently baked cookies still filled the air, mingling with the smell of fresh pine from the tree that sat in the bucket of rocks in the middle of the room. A small present was already wrapped and sitting beneath the decorated tree.

"Will the new kittens have their own star in the sky? When they are born?" Andy asked after a minute.

Andy looked up at Zach when he asked the

question and Zach froze. He didn't know anything about that night in Bethlehem. He wasn't able to answer any questions.

Fortunately, Jenny was there on the sofa. She shook her head. "The star was only for the Baby Jesus."

Lisa sighed. "That's why we have stars today."

"Well, we had stars before Christmas," Jenny said softly. "But none of them were as special as the Christmas star."

"It was the biggest, bestest star ever," Lisa said in satisfaction.

"My star is big, too," Andy said as he pointed to the tree that stood in the center of the living room. "It's that one."

Andy and Lisa had colored their stars. The folded foil stars had been marked with red highlighters and yellow highlighters. Some had flowers drawn on them. One had a horse. They each had a hole poked in their top for a piece of twine so they could be tied to the tree branches. The stars made the lopsided pine tree sparkle with reflected light from the red and green lights that were twined around the tree branches.

The star Andy pointed to had to be at least four inches across. It was so big it hung crooked on the tree branch. A yellow stick figure had been drawn on it with a big circle around its head.

Zach thought the stick figure must be an angel and the circle a halo.

"It's a beautiful star," Jenny agreed as she shifted the arm she had around the boy and gave him a quick hug.

Andy wiggled down from the sofa and walked over to Zach's chair. "Did you see my star?"

"I sure did," Zach assured the boy. "I think it's the best ever. And that's some angel you drew."

Zach could see Lisa roll her eyes from where she still sat on the sofa. "It's not an angel. It's you."

The girl might as well have thrown a thunderbolt at him. "Me? An angel?"

"It's a cowboy," Lisa said as she stood up and walked over to the tree. She touched the star and then looked at Zach. "See. There's the hat."

"You put me on your star?" Zach repeated stupidly as he looked down at Andy.

The boy was smiling. "I put Thunder, too— on the other one."

Andy went over and touched the star with the horse on it before turning to Zach. "Do you like them?"

"They're the best ever," Zach said as he cleared his throat and then blinked. A bit of smoke from the lantern must have got in his eye. "What a wonderful Christmas surprise."

Andy looked at Lisa and they both giggled.

"That's not your Christmas surprise," Lisa finally said. "We've got that planned for tomorrow morning."

Zach hadn't had the breath knocked out of him this completely since he had been bucked off Black Demon in Fargo last year. He knew his mouth was hanging open, but he couldn't close it.

"We can't tell you what it is," Andy warned. The boy danced in excitement. "It's a surprise."

"Well, I'll be," Zach finally managed to say. "A Christmas surprise for me."

Zach turned to Jenny. He admitted he was a little giddy. Usually the only Christmas gifts he ever got were bottles of booze. "They have a surprise for me."

Jenny had never been prouder of her children. They'd planned a Christmas surprise for a guest in their household without any prompting or guidance from her. Jenny thought about that for a minute, and her pride quickly turned to worry. Her children had planned a Christmas surprise for Zach without her input. That could spell disaster.

Not all men appreciated the same things that
children did, and Jenny knew that. Granted,
Zach had seemed genuinely touched by the
stars. But who knew if he'd react as well to
some wrinkled tie made out of paper or a cardboard belt buckle?

"I think maybe it's time for bed now,"
Jenny announced.

Even though both of her children sat with
pleased looks on their faces, Jenny was sure one
of them would tell her about their planned
surprise when she tucked them into bed. If she
knew what the big gift was, maybe she could
straighten a few of the corners or iron it or
something. She'd noticed that several of the
boxes in the corner of the living room looked
as if someone had gone through them this afternoon.

Well, Jenny thought, whatever it was, she
would do whatever she could to make it better.
If she only knew what it was. Unfortunately,
neither one of her children would budge, insist-
ing it was a Christmas-morning surprise and
surprises were secrets.

"Well, at least show me before you show it
to him. Okay?" Jenny pulled the covers up to
Lisa's chin and reminded herself to have her
scissors and glue handy in the morning. Maybe

she should also get out a needle and thread. "Is the surprise made out of cloth or paper?"

"Mom." Lisa rolled her eyes. "It's a surprise."

"I know, sweetie." Jenny bent down and kissed her daughter on the forehead. "I know."

Zach was in the kitchen, sitting at the table and stamping *PRIORITY* on a full yard of brown postal paper. He added a few green snowflakes drawn with one marker that still had ink in it. He decided right then that he needed to start carrying a bigger duffel. Either that or he'd have to tell Mrs. Brown she needed to carry more supplies in her postal bin. He wished he had glitter or velvet or even a red stamp that gave a holiday greeting instead of a postal message. And that was just the stuff at the bottom of his wish list.

Right now, he wished for a whole lot of things.

Ever since he'd seen that star, he'd wished he had time to go to Denver or Salt Lake or at least Billings to buy Christmas presents for this little family. He'd like to buy a princess doll and a tiara with real diamonds for Lisa. She could sell it when she wanted to go to college someday— and with a mind like hers she'd definitely want to go.

Then he'd buy a horse for Andy. And if a real horse would be too much trouble, he'd buy one of those electronic ones that they used in bars. He'd find one with a gentle setting. And, if he couldn't find one with a gentle setting, he'd buy the boy a carousel with a dozen horses to choose from.

And for Jenny—Zach stopped stamping and smiled—for Jenny he'd buy a full-length mink coat. Fake, of course, if she was bothered by the real thing. But something warm enough to weather the worst Montana storm her guide-book ever dreamed could hit.

He'd also buy her a tractor.

But Zach knew there was no time to travel and no clear roads even if there had been time. There was no way to get to the gifts he wanted to buy. So he'd just have to make do with what he had.

"They're in bed," Jenny announced as she stood in the doorway to the kitchen. She had brought the lantern into the kitchen before putting the children to bed, and its yellow light formed a circle around the table and Zach. The Christmas-tree lights had given off enough light for her to see Lisa and Andy to bed. Both children had promised to go to sleep quickly.

"They've had a busy day." Zach didn't know when he'd had a better day himself. He'd certainly never had a better day related to Christmas. He stopped stamping the brown paper and raised it up. "Do you think I should stamp this some more?"

"It looks good." Jenny had never seen a man so taken with Christmas. "I brought the wire hanger you wanted. And the strip of old towel."

Zach admired Jenny standing in the doorway. The red and green lights from the living room backed her silhouette, while the yellow light from the lantern played up the blond highlights in her hair. Her face looked dewy smooth and sculpted. Her eyelashes were thick, and he didn't think she was even wearing any mascara. The shadows hid her blue eyes, and they looked like an ocean at midnight.

Zach swallowed and forced himself to think of the presents he still had to make. The night promised to be even longer than the watch on his wrist indicated. "Thanks for bringing everything. I'd better get started."

Zach had taken his duffel into the kitchen. He'd found a few minutes during the day to slip into the laundry room and pound belt holes in the strip of leather he was planning to use in Andy's gift. The rest of the work would be quiet, and he could do it while everyone slept.

"You're sure you want to cut this up?" Jenny walked over to the counter where Zach had laid out the leg garter and picked it up. The lantern light made the rhinestones sparkle quietly. "This had to be expensive."

The black lace and velvet circle studded with rhinestones looked like something out of a classy department store rather than a vending machine. Jenny counted the stones. Fifteen. "These look real."

"The rubies are." Zach rolled the stamped postal paper up. He'd need the whole table for working. "There's only a couple of them. Of course, they're not high quality."

"And you're cutting this up?" Jenny looked at the garter more closely. Those rubies sure did look genuine. "You can't cut this up—not if they're real."

Jenny frowned. She didn't like the fact that Zach had bought something with actual jewels in it for his girlfriend. A garter was one thing, but jewels! Jewels meant commitment. Maybe Zach's relationship with the showgirl was more serious than he had let on. Of course, he did not owe Jenny any explanations about his relationships with women. Zach and her family were stranded together in a snowstorm. He didn't even want to be here. "I'm sure Patti would want the rubies even if you give them to her after Christmas."

"Ah, well, I don't know when I'll see her now. I mean, she expected me today so—" Zach didn't want to admit to Jenny that he'd lost all appetite for his Vegas vacation.

"Oh, and she won't know what's happened. She'll be worried."

"Not likely."

Jenny felt a little better. "She'll probably see the weather reports about a blizzard here. She'll know your trip might have been interrupted."

"Yeah." Zach didn't want to keep talking about Patti. He knew the showgirl wouldn't worry about him at all. "Do you have that hanger? I think that's the first thing to do—see if I can bend that into a likely shape." Zach looked up at Jenny. "Mind if I use your head to size it?"

"Huh?"

"The tiara." Zach took the metal hanger Jenny handed to him and ran his hands along it. "Good quality."

Jenny sat down at the table.

Zach stood up. This tiara-making business wasn't so bad. He realized he had every excuse in the world to touch Jenny's head. "Lisa's hair is the same color as yours. Very pretty."

"Thank you." Jenny felt warm—too warm

for a night like this. It was thirty degrees below zero outside tonight, and she knew for a fact that she kept the furnace thermometer set at sixty-five. She should be shivering from the cold instead of the heat—she barely felt Zach's hands as they circled the top of her head. Of course, it wasn't his hands that were bothering her. It was him. He was six feet of muscle standing behind her chair. She could feel the heat from his body. She wondered if he could feel her heart racing. "It's been quite a day."

"Mmm-hmm." Zach tried to keep his mind on the tiara instead of the fact that Jenny's hair was soft enough to kiss. And thick—her curls would scatter over a pillow like the petals of a sunflower. And to think he used to prefer long hair on his girlfriends.

What was he thinking? Zach pulled his hand back. Jenny wasn't his girlfriend. She wouldn't even kiss him. Well, he didn't think she'd kiss him. He hadn't asked again since this morning. And she was sitting awfully still in this dimly lit kitchen. He put his hand back, this time on her shoulder, and she didn't pull away. That had to be a good sign.

"Women—they say they can always change their minds, don't they?" Zach asked without thinking.

"Huh?" Jenny turned around to look at him. In the shadows her eyes were deep blue and unreadable.

"Ah…Lisa. You're sure she wants a tiara?" Zach could have kicked himself. He rode bucking horses, after all. He was always able to ride out of the chute when the bar was pulled back. He never wavered. He never hesitated. Until now.

Jenny turned back around, and Zach began to gently rub her shoulders. "Yeah, I'm sure. She's talked about it ever since we moved here. I wish I'd known sooner. I could have found one in a store in Los Angeles and brought it with us."

"Yeah."

Zach told himself a responsible, decent Santa would get on with making Christmas gifts and forget about the woman sitting in front of him. "And what do you want for Christmas?"

"Me?" Jenny laughed. "I've been working too hard to think about what I want."

"You need someone to help you."

Jenny leaned back into the man's hands. He was giving her a back rub. It felt wonderful. "I've been thinking of getting a dog."

"A dog?" Zach almost lost his rhythm in the back rub. That certainly put him in his place. He was losing his touch.

"Yeah, someone to chase the rabbits out of the garden come spring."

"You're planting a garden!" Zach had driven through this part of Montana last summer, when there hadn't been a foot of snow on the ground. "You'll need to put down a layer of topsoil first. The wind blew it all off a couple of years ago. Besides, you already have a cat."

"The guidebook didn't mention anything about topsoil." Jenny frowned as she turned around to look at Zach. "It said I could grow anything. And cats and dogs can get along."

When pigs can fly, Zach thought. But he didn't say it. "Potatoes might grow," he said instead. He pressed harder against Jenny's left shoulder. "They don't take much topsoil."

"But I want snap peas and roses. Sort of an English garden. And some tomatoes."

"Oh." Zach moved over to the right shoulder.

Jenny felt as if her shoulders were putty. Warm, melting putty. Zach was massaging them with the palms of his hands. Then Zach moved his hands to the base of the back of Jenny's neck.

Jenny held back the moan that purred deep in her throat. "How'd you ever get so good at this?" Jenny regretted the question as soon as she asked it. A single man like Zach learned to give massages for only one reason.

"My horse," Zach answered. Now, why had Jenny stiffened up like that? There, that was better. "He had a leg injury."

"Ah, good," Jenny sighed.

"He didn't think so."

"No, I don't suppose he would."

The massage left Jenny relaxed and energized both at the same time. "I should help you with the presents."

"We've got time." Zach had never felt this content in all his life. Not when he'd bought his first horse. Not when he'd first won the Pro-Championship title. Not when he'd signed the contract with the Ranger cereal company. Not ever. "I like being here with you."

Jenny heard the words Zach whispered. Suddenly she didn't care that he was a man who was just traveling through. "I like you, too."

"Like as in like, or…?" Zach didn't want to shatter the quiet of the evening by making a false move.

Jenny stood up and turned to face Zach. There were only three inches between them. Then there were two. Then…

Jenny figured some women live their whole

lives and never have a kiss like this one. It curled her toes and made her breath stop in her throat. She would have swooned, but mothers with two young children did not swoon.

"Hmm." Zach still had the taste of her lips on his tongue. He was reluctant to let go.

"I think—"

"Don't think."

"I think I need to wrap the Christmas presents."

Ah, Christmas. Christmas had given Zach trouble for years. Strangely enough, for the first time he didn't mind so much. "You can stamp while I finish up on the other presents."

Jenny not only stamped enough brown postal paper to wrap the gifts, she drew red bells on them. So what if the bells grew to look a little like hearts? It was Christmas, after all, and Christmas was a time for wishes and dreams.

It was even, she told herself firmly, a time for dreams that had no hope of ever coming true. She knew Zach "Lightning" Lucas was just passing through. She knew he wished he were in Las Vegas. She knew he hated Christmas and was just being kind to her and her children. She knew he hadn't been to church in ages. But, even knowing all that, she couldn't help smiling when he walked into the unheated laundry room and came back with the mistletoe in his hand. "We could use this for decorations on the packages."

"It's a pity to waste it," Jenny said. She watched the slow smile spread across Zach's face as she added, "After all, it is Christmas Eve."

Jenny floated to bed that night. She'd had one special night. She'd been kissed. She'd been hugged. She'd been listened to by someone who paid attention.

If she had to keep reminding herself that it wouldn't last forever, that is what she would do. After all, once Christmas was gone, winter would be long and cold. Her heart would have time to forget all about the cowboy.

Jenny listened until she heard the door to the house close. Zach was on his way to the barn.

The night was full dark when Zach made his way out to the barn. He carried an old aluminum pan filled with milk made from powder. He had a small bag of crackers stuffed in his coat pocket. He figured he'd have to start the fire small tonight so that the milk didn't burn on top of the wood stove. That cat was a lot of trouble.

He'd probably have to stir the milk while it

heated. Which was okay. He'd already decided to light the kerosene lamp for a while so he could read about the Christmas story in the Bible he'd seen earlier in that room. He wanted to be able to answer Andy's questions when he asked them. And even if the boy was finished with his questions, Zach wasn't. There had to be more to the story than that one night in Bethlehem.

## Chapter Ten

Could kisses give anyone a hangover?

Jenny sat in her bed and wondered how she could feel so bad on Christmas morning. Well, technically it wasn't morning yet, she comforted herself as she looked out the window in her bedroom. It was deep gray outside. The wind had stopped blowing. She had a good half hour before she had to get up and pretend everything was well with the world.

It was Merry Christmas time. Hugs and Santa time.

Jenny wanted to crawl into a dark pit and stay there until spring. But—she squinted at the illuminated clock by her bed—in nineteen minutes, she would smile. And she would pretend that everything was wonderful, even if she had to crawl to the Christmas tree on her hands and knees. Christmas was a special time of the year for children, and Jenny was determined to add to her children's cheer and not take away from it.

It wasn't her children's fault that Jenny had gone crazy last night and thrown caution to the wind. And crazy it was. She'd fallen in love with a man who was only passing through—a man who had not even meant to end up in her house and would have left if the snow had not left them snowbound. He had only been there to deliver a package, after all. He was the mailman. And not even the regular mailman. He wanted to spend Christmas with a showgirl instead of a widow and her two young children. What had she been thinking? The man didn't even believe in God. They clearly had no future.

Jenny felt around in the semidarkness for the bottle of water she kept by her bed. Now, if she only had an aspirin. Or two. She winced. Make that four.

Jenny heard the door to the kitchen open. Zach was back.

Zach was miserable. He would never be able to look at another Christmas card again. Or even a postal stamp—Fragile, Return to Sender,

Priority—they would all be signals to him to count his shortcomings in the future.

He was a grown man. He should have known he would have to pay the price for those kisses last night. Never before had he so deeply regretted the kind of man he was.

He'd read enough of the Bible last night to have a glimmer of the kind of man Jenny deserved. Zach wasn't that man. If he had any clue as to how to be a godly, family man, he would take a nail and permanently tack that piece of mistletoe to the doorway of this house. And then he'd beg Jenny to marry him.

But he wasn't good at relationships. He didn't even know how much he didn't know. Maybe when he finished reading the Bible, he'd have a list. But, right now, all he knew was that his list of shortcomings was long. And it wasn't fair to Jenny to pretend otherwise. It certainly wasn't fair to the kids.

Sure, Zach admitted, he'd done all right for a day or two. He'd filled in for Stephen, who should have been here with them. Anyone could follow a good act for a few minutes. It was like riding on a bronc that had been winded by the previous rider. It wasn't a fair test. And it wouldn't take long for Jenny to realize he was a fake.

Zach didn't relish seeing the disappointment

in her eyes. He would have to leave. But before he left, he owed them a merry Christmas. He was, for better or for worse, Santa Claus.

Zach was in the laundry room, snapping his white beard into place, when he heard the first whisper. It sounded like Andy. The answer that came sounded like Lisa. Zach hurriedly put the Santa hat on his head. He'd already put the rest of the outfit on—even that belt with the lights.

Then he walked into the living room.

Speaking of lights—Zach walked over until he could reach the battery switch to turn on the Christmas-tree lights. The tree glowed in the early morning light, casting red and green shadows all around the living room.

The tree sat in the middle of the living room, and the lights danced on all four walls. Zach's eyes were drawn to the bulletin board that he'd seen earlier. He'd avoided the pictures on the board yesterday, but now—knowing his hours with this family were limited—he went over to look at the pictures.

He had to smile. There was a photo of Andy dressed as a pumpkin for some reason. There was Lisa in a frilly white dress and almost no teeth. And the zoo—there must have been four or five pictures of the children at the zoo. Andy by the elephants. Lisa by a giraffe. And the beach—there were so many pictures at the beach. In one of them, Jenny was building a sand castle with Andy. That picture was crooked. Lisa must have snapped it.

Zach wondered how many men's hearts were broken on Christmas morning. He wanted to give so much, and he had so little to give.

"What?" Jenny's voice carried from her bedroom. The children were clearly in with her, and a quiet rumble of whispers followed Jenny's first outburst. Zach couldn't make out any of the words, but he could tell a heated discussion was taking place behind the closed door.

Zach wondered if he was about to get his surprise. It sounded like some surprise. He only hoped the wrapped packages under the tree would be sufficient to repay the children for the amount of convincing they were doing. It sounded like an uphill battle was being fought in there.

He wondered what they were giving him that their mother so clearly disapproved of. It must be something like a knife. Mothers always disapproved of knives—as they should. But that couldn't be it. Jenny wouldn't care if he had a knife.

Maybe—and the thought didn't sit well with him—the children had decided to give him something that had belonged to their father and Jenny couldn't part with it. That made sense. Some favorite shirt or tie. Well, she didn't need to worry about him. He would quietly return anything they gave him that had sentimental value.

The voices went silent and then Zach saw Lisa's head poke out of the partially opened door. She looked around and saw him.

"You need to go sit on the sofa," the girl directed him, before giving a worried look back into the bedroom. "We're almost ready."

Andy came out first and ran across the room to settle on the sofa next to Zach. Zach put his arm around the boy before he looked down at Andy's hair. A tiny white feather was sitting on top of the boy's head.

"Dum-da-dum," Lisa trumpeted as she stood in the open doorway.

What on earth…? Zach watched Lisa sneeze. She had a dozen tiny white feathers flying around her. They floated around her before settling to the floor.

Zach decided the children must be giving him a chicken for Christmas. A live chicken. That's all it could be with those feathers. But where had they kept a chicken? There certainly weren't any birds in the barn.

"Dum-da-dum," Lisa repeated as she stepped to the side of the door and waved her arm for someone to come onstage.

What on earth…? Zach's first thought was that there must be a truckload of chickens inside Jenny's bedroom. Tiny white feathers floated everywhere as Jenny stood in the doorway in her—Zach took a second look and started to grin—Jenny was in a red-and white cheerleader's outfit.

"It's a showgirl," Andy whispered.

Zach grinned like a fool. "That it is."

"You told them a showgirl was a cheerleader with feathers in her hair," Jenny accused him as she stood in the doorway to the bedroom. She held a pom-pom in each hand and had an exasperated smile on her face. "Lisa even sacrificed her goose-down pillow so they'd have feathers."

"It works for me," Zach said. He couldn't take his eyes off Jenny. She stood there daring him to laugh. Her blue eyes glinted with steel. Her hair was sprayed stiff and covered with feathers. She was absolutely amazing.

"We have a cheer," Lisa announced as she motioned Andy to join her. "A Christmas cheer."

Zach saw Jenny close her eyes in resignation.

"One…two…three," Lisa counted off before she added, "Now."

The three voices blended. They spelled out the words. "M-E-R-R-Y C-H-R-I-S-T-M-A-S— Merry Christmas to you!"

Jenny kicked her leg up and shook her pom-poms. Lisa and Andy just screamed.

"Did you like it?" Andy asked eagerly before anyone else had regained their breath.

"I liked it a lot," Zach answered. Even if he lived to be a hundred, he would never receive a better Christmas surprise than this. "It's the best present ever."

"That's not all," Lisa screeched as she ran to the kitchen and came back with the camera. She handed the camera to Zach before rushing back to the doorway. "You get to take a picture of us, too."

Zach's eyes were blurry and his hands shook. But he snapped two pictures all the same. Now it really was the best Christmas gift possible. He had pictures of Jenny and the kids.

Jenny watched as Zach carefully set the pictures aside to develop. Well, he'd been a good sport about it. Lisa and Andy were still trembling with excitement, although she noticed their attention had moved from Zach to the wrapped packages lying under the tree.

"Did Santa come?" Andy finally asked softly.

Zach swallowed. "Well now, let's see."

"Do we have kittens yet?" Lisa asked.

"I don't think so. Not yet," Zach said. He'd put the warm milk in a dish by his door and it had been gone in the morning, but he hadn't seen the cat.

Since there were no kittens, both children went back to the presents.

It was an hour later before Jenny was able to convince everyone they needed to eat some breakfast. Lisa was pirouetting around the living room, dipping and twirling with her tiara. Andy was proudly strutting with the Stetson hat Zach had given him and the cowboy belt.

Jenny herself had been dumbfounded—Zach had given her his sheepskin coat. She shouldn't accept it. Jenny knew he didn't have another coat with him and even though he claimed the Santa suit would keep him warm until he could buy another one, she still shouldn't take his coat. But she couldn't resist.

It wasn't because the coat was warm and she'd realized winter would be much colder than her guidebook had indicated. No, the reason she couldn't refuse was because when she had the coat around her, she felt as though Zach was with her. The coat carried the woodsy smell of him. It just plain comforted her. And she had a feeling she would need some comforting even before the day was gone.

"I need to have cereal for breakfast," Andy said after Jenny mentioned the meal. Andy swung his twine rope around. "I want some of the cereal that real cowboys eat."

"We might have to eat the cereal without milk," Jenny said. She didn't feel like leaving the living room just yet. "Unless you want milk made from powder."

"Would a cowboy eat that?" Andy asked as he looked up at Zach.

"Cowboys eat whatever's set before them," Zach said. "They get hungry out on the trail."

Andy nodded.

"But I don't know what princesses eat." Lisa stopped pirouetting. Her tiara tilted on her head, but she managed to look regal. "Andy can have cereal, but what will I have?"

"Peas," Zach answered. He was sitting on the sofa telling himself he'd never known a single moment in his life when he had been happier. Watching the kids play. Seeing Jenny wrapped in his coat. It was a perfect moment in time. "Canned peas."

"What?" Lisa looked as him suspiciously. She even walked over to him and leaned on his knee. "You're teasing me."

Zach brushed a feather out of her hair. "You've heard of *The Princess and the Pea.*"

"But that wasn't breakfast, silly." Lisa giggled and rolled her eyes. "That was for her mattress."

"Is that right?" Zach watched Lisa laugh and shake her head. Another white feather floated to the floor. "You mean she sleeps on her vegetables?"

The sun had come up and was shining in the windows. The lights were still steadily lit on the Christmas tree, but the sunshine from outside dulled their glow.

"No, she doesn't," Lisa protested. "Nobody sleeps on vegetables."

Zach gave an exaggerated shrug. "I don't know. Kings and queens do strange things sometimes. I figure princesses might, as well."

"You could have toast and jam," Jenny offered. "And I could fix you some tea the way the English make it."

"I could be an English princess," Lisa agreed, and then leaned even more on Zach's knee as she looked at him. "And you can be my servant."

"Me?" Zach lifted his eyebrows and smiled at the girl. "Well, I guess you're right. A princess does need a servant or two. I would be delighted to serve you breakfast, madame."

"Not madame, it's Princess Lisa."

"Indeed it is, Princess Lisa."

Zach decided to serve everyone breakfast when they were all seated at the table. He put a kitchen towel over his arm and a falsetto tone in his voice. He poured from the right and removed from the left. He made the children laugh and Jenny roll her eyes in merriment.

And then, when Zach almost had his back turned, he saw Jenny twist the cereal box around so she wouldn't have to see his picture on the back of the box.

"A problem with the box? I could remove it from the table if you like." Zach could hear the hurt in his own voice. No wonder men didn't like to be vulnerable—especially over breakfast.

"It's not—" Jenny started to explain. "It's not you. It's me."

"How can it be you and not me? It's my picture on the box." He might be hurt, but he wasn't brain-dead. No one here owed him anything. Jenny didn't need to spare his feelings. Still, Zach didn't want his heart to bleed in front of the children. Especially not on Christmas Day. He forced himself to smile. "Not that it matters. More toast anyone?"

Jenny took a deep breath and closed her eyes. "I used to talk to your picture."

"What?" Zach had picked up the empty toast plate, and now he held it suspended.

Jenny opened her eyes. "I used to talk to your picture on the back of the cereal box."

"Really?"

"I was lonely," Jenny said defensively. "People pick up strange habits when they're lonely. I mean, it's not as if I knew you then."

"Really?" Zach had never thought of anyone talking to his picture before. "Really?"

"It's not that big of a deal. It's only a cereal box."

Zach started to smile. He almost started to whistle. "No problem. Anyone want more toast?"

Learning that someone made a habit of talking to your picture could boost a man's ego, Zach thought to himself all through the rest of the morning. It made twenty games of rope-the-foot possible with a little cowboy, as the boy learned to twirl his rope. It made ten dances with a princess possible, complete with nine bows and one beheading for displeasing the royal one. It even carried Zach through peeling potatoes and basting the Christmas ham.

It wasn't until Christmas dinner was finished

that it occurred to Zach that Jenny might have talked to a box of detergent if it had been sitting on her table when she was so desperate. A woman whose beloved husband was sick would talk to anything rather than confess her worries to her husband.

"I'm sure he was a very special man—your Stephen," Zach said. Christmas, after all, was a time to think of others rather than yourself. Zach wanted her to know she could still talk to him. "It must be hard to have your first Christmas without him."

Zach and Jenny were sitting alone at the table. The children had eaten and fled into the living room to play. The blizzard had ended sometime last night and the sunlight coming inside now was so strong and warm that no candles were needed. The frost had melted on the windows. It was the middle of the afternoon.

Jenny took a deep breath. She owed it to Zach to tell him the truth—the whole miserable lot of it. But where did she start? "Stephen and I would have been married for ten years this coming February."

"What date?"

"Huh?"

"The date. What date did you get married?"

"February fourteenth, Valentine's Day, although I don't see—"

Zach's shoulders slumped. He was right. This Stephen had been a charmer. What woman wouldn't want to get married on Valentine's Day? How was another man ever supposed to compete with that? "You must have had some memorable anniversaries."

"Memorable is right." Jenny hadn't realized for two years that the reason Stephen had been so intent that they marry on Valentine's Day was so he wouldn't have to remember a separate anniversary date. Even with the added help, he hadn't remembered their anniversary for the past five years. "But that's not what I want to say."

"I know you loved him." The kitchen was warm and smelled good. Sunshine streamed into the room, and Zach could hear the children playing in the living room. He wanted to wrap the memory of this moment around him tight so that he could pull it out on some lonely night in the future and remember the time he'd been part of a family.

There was a soft ticking, and it took a minute before Zach realized what it was—he was hearing the clock. The electricity was back on.

Jenny swallowed. "Love is a complicated thing sometimes."

"I'd expect so," Zach lied. He didn't find love complicated at all. Painful, yes. Complicated, no.

"It's not always—" Jenny began, and then paused.

The telephone rang.

"Service is back," Zach muttered. He supposed it wasn't fair, but he wouldn't have minded if the electricity stayed off for another week. Especially not if another storm moved in and kept them all snowbound together. But he'd known since morning that the snow outside was melting. Sure, the road still had a buildup of snow on it, but he might be able to push his way through in the postal truck this afternoon.

"Hello," Jenny answered the phone. "Oh, hi, Mrs. Hargrove. I can't thank you enough for— oh, yes, he's here." Jenny paused, listening. "No, no he hasn't shown up yet. Yes, I'll call you then." Another pause. "No, no, it was no problem. It was good to have him here. Yes, I'll see you tomorrow, then."

It didn't take a snowdrift to freeze Zach's heart. He already heard a distant roar coming toward the house.

Jenny hung up and looked at Zach. "Mrs. Hargrove sent the county snowplow out to plow our road."

"I didn't think they'd work on Christmas. Isn't that overtime?"

"Double time, but they had to do it. We have the postal truck, and tomorrow is a mail day."

Couldn't the mail just wait for a day? Zach thought. Or maybe a week. Even a month would be okay. "So this is it."

Jenny nodded. "You'll have to drive the postal truck back."

But you can come back then, Jenny thought. There's nothing that says you can't come back. We haven't had nearly enough time to…to what? she asked herself. More time would only add to the heartbreak if he was going to leave, anyway.

"I'm going to leave the reindeer horns and the lights," Zach said. He could hardly speak. How did a man leave when every atom of his being wanted to stay? "Mrs. Hargrove or Charley can pick them up later."

Jenny nodded. "Mrs. Hargrove told me how grateful she was you drove for Charley that last day. Otherwise, he would be here and they would have been apart for Christmas."

"No problem."

Zach willed his legs to move. He could hear the snowplow clearly outside now. There were no more excuses to stay. But he still sat.

"You'll be in Vegas late tomorrow." Jenny

twisted a knot in the napkin she held in her hand. Zach had never pretended to be anything other than a cowboy out looking for a good time. Even she knew a widow with two little kids wasn't a good time.

"Yeah," Zach lied. He didn't know where he was going. He didn't care. But he had no appetite anymore for Vegas. A grieving man didn't go to Vegas. He'd rather find a deserted hotel somewhere in the open spaces of Utah and lick his wounds for a few weeks. He might even take the Bible out of the drawer in the hotel room and read up on what a wretched man he was.

A man's boots stomped on the porch before a loud knock came and a call was made through the kitchen door. "I'm the snowplow man. Out from Miles City."

There was a moment of silence.

"He'll want a cup of coffee," Jenny finally said as she stood to open the door.

"I'd best say goodbye to the kids." Zach stood, as well. The dream was over.

## Chapter Eleven

"You must be Zach," Mrs. Hargrove said as she opened the door to her house. The warm smell of roasting turkey came floating out into the cold air behind her. "I hear you were one popular Santa Claus. Why, Charley got calls—"

"Calls?" Zach's heart started to pound. He stopped scraping the snow off his boots and just stood there. The snow plow man had told Zach that Charley would be at his fiancée's house for dinner, and it hadn't taken much to find the place.

Mrs. Hargrove nodded. "Mrs. Goussley left three messages telling him how much the cats missed you already and what a great Santa you were."

"Oh." Zach grunted as he started scraping his boots again. The cats. It was always the cats.

The one out in the Collinses' barn hadn't even shown itself when he went out to pack up his duffel. Christmas had got the best of him again. Next Christmas he wasn't taking any chances. He'd head to a deserted island, maybe some-place off the Alaskan coastline. Or maybe Iceland. No one went to Iceland in the winter. And if they did, they didn't bring their cats.

"And, of course, the candy canes were a hit," the older woman continued as she accepted the bag from Zach that held the Santa costume. "They always are."

Mrs. Hargrove was just as Zach had pictured her. She had bouncy gray hair and a mouth that didn't stop chatting. Her bright eyes welcomed him like he belonged.

How was she to know he didn't belong anywhere?

"I suppose Thunder is well enough to travel," Zach said.

"Well, yes, but you don't want to head out this afternoon. You won't make it to a town with a hotel before dark. Besides, Charley has a spare room at his place, and we'd love to have you join us for dinner. There's nothing like a fresh turkey dinner with all the trim-mings."

Mrs. Hargrove was the picture of hospitality

with a red-checked apron hanging over a cotton dress. She had pearl earrings on her ears and orthopedic shoes on her feet. She was looking at him as if he were a long-lost friend.

Zach forced himself to smile. "Thanks, but I'll be moving on. I might make it into Wyoming before nightfall."

"Well, if you're sure." A tiny frown settled on Mrs. Hargrove's forehead. "But I know Charley would like to thank you, and he's not here yet."

"No need to thank me."

"We've got pie, too. Apple and cherry. I've never known a cowboy to turn down a piece of homemade pie."

"That's kind of you, but I'd best be moving on."

"Well, all right then." Mrs. Hargrove reached behind herself to get a sweater and stepped out onto the porch. "Let me just go park the postal truck in its spot."

"I can move it if you tell me where it goes."

"It's easier just to show you," Mrs. Hargrove said with a wave of her hand as she marched off the porch.

"A sweater's not warm enough," Zach called after her. Oh, well, Zach thought, if she didn't care, who was he to make a big deal out

of it? He was through taking care of people—
and cats—who didn't listen to him, anyway.

Zach followed Mrs. Hargrove out to the
postal truck. He'd parked the truck at the curb
in front of her house.

"Oh, what's this?" Mrs. Hargrove had
already opened the door and leaned into the
truck. She reached out for the photographs
that Zach had laid out on the dash.

Zach winced. He'd taken the pictures out so
he could look at them as he bounced along the
country roads back into Dry Creek. "I'll just
pack them up. Got my duffel in back, too."

Mrs. Hargrove stepped back, holding all four
pictures. She squinted in the sunlight as she
tilted the photographs up so she could see them
better. "Why, aren't those nice?"

"Yeah." Zach swallowed. He didn't know
what to say. Not that there was anything to say.
A picture was just a picture.

Mrs. Hargrove looked closely at each
picture. Zach didn't have to see the pictures to
know what she saw. A picture of Jenny as his
showgirl. A picture of Andy roping his foot. A
picture of him dancing with Princess Lisa. A
picture of him and the children dragging the
Christmas tree up from the coulee.

"Well," Mrs. Hargrove said softly as she

lowered the pictures and turned curious eyes toward Zach. "Looks as though you had some Christmas."

Zach grunted. "I was just doing what I could to make sure they had a good Christmas."

"I can see that."

"Anyone would have done the same." Zach held out his hand. He wasn't going anywhere without his pictures. "They're good kids."

"Uh-huh," Mrs. Hargrove agreed. She didn't hand over the pictures, though. "I don't think I've ever seen the kids like this—laughing and being silly."

"Well, it's Christmas. You know how kids are at Christmas."

"I suppose." Mrs. Hargrove took another hard look at him as she finally handed him the pictures.

The sun had warmed the air considerably, but it was still too cold to stand outside and talk. Zach hoped that fact would encourage the woman to go back inside. "They're just missing their father."

"The kids?" Mrs. Hargrove seemed surprised. "Did they talk about him?"

Zach shuffled. He hadn't meant to get into a conversation about the man. "Well, no, but you gotta figure he was a good father. Good husband, too. They got married on Valentine's Day, you know."

"No, I didn't know."

Zach knew it was time to go. There were only a couple of hours of daylight left, and he wanted to get closer to the Wyoming border before pulling off the interstate for the night. But his mouth just kept talking.

"Must have been tough when he died," Zach added. What was wrong with him? Then he knew what he wanted to say. He knew the question he wanted to ask someone. "Wonder what made him so special, anyway?"

Mrs. Hargrove looked Zach over once again. He felt her gaze on him. She wasn't unkind about it. She was obviously just thinking.

"What makes you think he was special?" Mrs. Hargrove finally asked.

"I figure he was a pillar of the church or something," Zach stumbled.

"I don't think so. Not from what little Jenny has said."

"Well…I…" Zach stammered. Of course the man was special. "The kids are such good kids, and Jenny—well, Jenny is wonderful."

Mrs. Hargrove nodded. "Funny thing, though. Jenny never talks about her late husband."

"Well, no, but…"

"Kids don't, either."

Zach was silent. Come to think of it, the kids didn't say much about their father.

"And did you ever see those pictures she's got hanging on the wall in the living room?"

Zach smiled and nodded. "They liked the zoo."

Mrs. Hargrove nodded, too. "Ever wonder why there's no pictures of the father there?"

The silence cracked over Zach's head. Mrs. Hargrove was right. There were no pictures of Stephen. "What do you suppose that means?"

Mrs. Hargrove shrugged. "I don't know for sure."

"You think it might not have been so perfect—" Zach cleared his throat. "I mean, do you think a man like me could have a chance? I know I'm not the kind of man Jenny deserves. I've been reading about it all in the Bible and—"

"You've been reading the Bible?"

"Well, I had to stay up and heat milk for the cat, anyway, so I thought I'd take a look."

"And?"

"Some of it's too good to be true. At least, for someone like me, but—"

"The Bible is for everyone."

Zach frowned. Could that be? That didn't seem right.

"If you want to spend some time learning about the Bible, Charley and I would be glad to help you with it. Like I said, he's got a spare room over at his place and there's no lack of odd jobs around for a man willing to work. You could stay a while in Dry Creek. See how things go."

"You'd do that for me?"

Mrs. Hargrove nodded. "I'd do that for the man who can make those kids laugh like that."

"I'm not Jerry Seinfeld or anything. I'm not naturally funny."

"That's what makes it so special." Mrs. Hargrove smiled. "They were happy, not entertained."

"You think there might be hope for me and Jenny then?"

"I'm not the one you need to ask."

Zach figured there was a silly smile on his face, but he couldn't stop the grin from spreading. "Mind if I borrow the postal truck again? I'll be back in a few hours."

Mrs. Hargrove grinned back at him as she handed him the keys.

"Tell Charley I'll pick Thunder up later."

"Don't worry. That old horse of yours will be fine in the barn out at the Nelson place."

The road back to Jenny's house had just as many bumps as it had the first time Zach had ridden over it. The difference was that this time he grinned a little more at each bump he drove over.

Jenny thought she heard someone drive up to her house, but she wasn't sure. She and the children had been sitting on the sofa with blankets snuggled around them. They'd been out in the barn earlier, but they couldn't find the cat so they came back into the house. Jenny had offered to read to them, but both kids seemed to just want to sit and be quiet.

"I think someone is here," Jenny said softly as she untangled her arms from the blankets.

"Tell them to go away," Andy muttered. "We don't want nobody."

"This is Montana," Jenny chided her son gently as she stood up. "Neighbors are important and will always be welcome in our house."

"If it's a stranger, you should be careful," Lisa advised glumly. "It's not just snakes you have to watch for around here."

"I'll be careful," Jenny said as she started to walk toward the kitchen. "It's probably just the snowplow guy again."

Jenny had to step around the Christmas tree to get to the kitchen. The batteries had died on the tree lights, and the stars didn't sparkle anymore. Andy's hat sat forgotten beside the tree. Lisa's tiara was next to it.

Christmas this year had been both the best ever and the worst ever for her little family.

The sun had melted most of the frost in the small window of the outside kitchen door. But the afternoon had faded and the light had never been good on that side of the house. She saw a shape, but she could not tell who it was. She squinted, anyway—those shoulders reminded her of—not that it would be him.

Jenny opened the door. What in the world—?

Jenny tried to form a word, but couldn't for a full minute. Then it occurred to her that many things could explain why this particular man was standing on her porch. "Forget something?"

Zach smiled. "I guess I did."

"Let me know where it is and I'll go get it." Jenny knew it was rude to leave someone standing on the porch, but she didn't want her children to know he was here. He'd only break their hearts two minutes later when he left again.

"Well, I don't quite know where it is." Zach tried smiling harder. His smile was often called charming by women.

There was no smile in return. "We only have the five rooms. And the barn, of course."

Zach looked at Jenny. She didn't exactly look welcoming. In fact, she looked as if she was barely tolerating his presence. Her eyes were guarded. She wasn't smiling. She hadn't invited him into the house and it was cold outside.

All in all, Zach conceded, it didn't look good. But a man didn't ride wild horses because he believed in taking the safe route. Zach reached up and ran his hands around the side brim of the Stetson hat sitting on his head. It was the same gesture he used when he was ready to start a rodeo ride.

"It's more of a question than anything."

"Oh?"

"When you talked to my face on that cereal box, what did you talk about?"

Jenny could hear Lisa and Andy running toward the kitchen. She didn't have much time. "Is this some market-research question? You think your sponsor would like to know? Maybe they'll find some small demographic niche of women who are crazy enough to talk to cereal boxes?"

The footsteps entered the kitchen.

"Mr. Lightning!"

"Santa!"

Two pairs of feet ran to the door and planted themselves beside Jenny.

"You're back!"

"You came!"

Now, this was a better welcome, Zach thought as he looked down at the kids. "Hi, there. Mind if I talk to your mom for a minute?"

"Sure," the two voices answered.

But no feet moved. Three pairs of eyes kept looking at him.

"Alone." Zach swallowed.

"Maybe you could go pick out the books you want me to read to you tonight," Jenny suggested.

"Okay," Lisa said, and started back to the living room. The girl nudged Andy to follow her.

Zach waited until the children were in the living room. "I'm not asking about the cereal box because I care about marketing. I want to know what you were thinking and feeling. I want to know why you don't have any pictures of Stephen on your bulletin board."

"Stephen?" Jenny paused. This was about Stephen?

"Was it because it was too painful for you to have any pictures of him around?"

"No," Jenny answered. "It's just that we didn't have any pictures. Not ones like that. I mean, we have a couple of formal shots—he needed one for a business thing once. But that was taken at a studio."

"Was the man camera shy?"

"Stephen? No."

"Then why don't you have any pictures?"

Jenny suddenly felt very tired. She'd never complained about Stephen. Never complained about him to anyone. She'd told herself she was protecting him. But now she wondered if she was only protecting herself.

There was such a long pause Zach wondered if Jenny was ever going to answer him.

"Because he was never with us," Jenny finally admitted. She needed to tell someone the truth about her life. "When we went to the zoo, he went fishing with some buddies of his. When we went to the beach, he went to a ball game with some other friends."

"So he wasn't some kind of superfather?"

"Stephen? No. He was barely a father at all."

Zach was beginning to have hope. Maybe he'd do all right as a father. But there was something even more important he needed to know.

"And as a husband? How was he as a husband?"

Jenny looked up at Zach. She saw longing for the children and for her in his eyes. She had never realized until now that Stephen's lack of interest in being a husband only added to his lack of interest in being a father. The two weren't separate. A man who would make a good husband to her would also make a good father to the children.

Especially, she thought to herself, if it was this man standing before her. She looked at him carefully. She could see the fear in his eyes. The drawn tension around his lips. All pretense was gone from his face. He was letting her see his insecurities and his longings.

Jenny reached up and caressed Zach's cheek briefly. She needed to let him see her as well. All her fears. Her defeats. Her tiredness. "He never loved me."

Jenny closed her eyes. There, she'd said it aloud. Stephen had never loved her.

A moment passed before Jenny realized her fears had not come true. Telling someone the truth about her and Stephen did not cause a crushing blackness in her heart. Instead, her heart felt lighter than it had in years.

Zach reached up and covered Jenny's hand with his. "He was a fool."

"I really tried to make him care." Jenny let Zach draw her into his arms.

"He didn't deserve you," Zach whispered. "You deserve someone better—"

Jenny opened her mouth to speak.

"No, don't answer yet. Hear me out." Zach

held her quietly and talked in her ear. He'd never had such an important moment in his life. Every word counted. "I grew up in a family of loners. I'm not the man for you yet. But I'm going to stay in Dry Creek for a while. I have some studying and thinking to do. I'm not sure how it will all end up. I'm not asking you to wait for me to figure it all out. I just want you to know."

Jenny opened her mouth again to speak. She couldn't think of what to say. "I can't—"

"Shhh," Zach said as he released her. "You don't need to answer yet. Just pretend I came back out to ask about the cat."

"We can't find the cat. The kids looked and looked." Jenny stood back and looked up at his face.

Zach smiled down at her. He needed to find out some answers before he was ready. But if there was any mercy left in God's heart at all, he wanted it. "If she's had the kittens, she probably doesn't want anyone to know just yet. Sometimes newborn things need time. Have you fed her this afternoon?"

Jenny shook her head. "I told the kids we'd take some more warm milk out to her later."

"I'll go with you," Zach offered. "She's used to me by now."

Fifteen minutes later, they were all walking to the barn. Andy was holding one of Zach's hands and Lisa was holding on to a loop in the man's sheepskin coat, which Jenny had loaned back to him, so Zach had his other hand free to carry the pan of milk. Both children were asking questions about the kittens they hoped to find.

Jenny smiled to herself as she walked with them. They were all used to Zach. But she knew it wasn't time for her to make a decision about him yet. She would need to know it was right in her mind and in her soul before she could commit to another man. She was glad he hadn't pushed for a decision.

He said he was the one who needed time to be ready for her, but she needed time to ready her heart for someone new as well. It might or might not be Zach. She didn't know if Zach would even want to be with her and the kids when he was done thinking about everything. All she could do was trust that God knew the man's heart.

Zach opened the barn door and they heard a tiny meow.

"It's a kitty," Lisa whispered.

The mother cat hissed at Zach when he put the pan of warm milk down.

"She's not ready for company yet," Zach said

as he guided the children back to the barn door. "Sometimes we have to be patient."

Zach looked at Jenny when he said the last, and she nodded. Her heart filled with hope. He was asking her to wait.

## Chapter Twelve

Jenny was helping Mrs. Hargrove plan her wedding. They were measuring the space at the front of the church so they would know how much room there would be for flowers. Lately, every Thursday at this time, the older woman had asked for Jenny's help for a few hours while Lisa was in school. Since the pastor's wife had asked if she could sketch Andy for a painting at the same time, Jenny was glad to help. She was beginning to wonder if the stress of planning a formal wedding wasn't too much for the older woman.

Jenny was trying to be quiet because the pastor was having a session in his office. No doubt it was Zach's session. She supposed Mrs. Hargrove liked to work while those sessions were going on because Charley was meeting with Zach and the pastor, too.

"I wonder if they're getting anyplace," Jenny said softly as she nodded her head toward the pastor's door.

"Charley says Zach is just making sure of things," Mrs. Hargrove said firmly.

Jenny held up one end of the tape measure and pressed it to the wall. "Are you sure we shouldn't measure for the candles, too?"

Mrs. Hargrove was halfway across the room from Jenny, holding the tape taut and taking a measurement. "Charley's the one who mentioned candles."

"If we knew where he might want them, we could take any measurements you need today," Jenny suggested. She didn't know how many different ways they could measure the church. Over the past couple of weeks, she'd helped the older woman measure the church space for flowers, for attendants, for banners and for aisle walking. And it never seemed as though any of the measurements they took were the right ones for any other addition to the wedding plans.

Not that Jenny minded spending time with Mrs. Hargrove. In fact, she had started looking forward to their measuring sessions.

A roar of disbelief sounded from the pastor's office, and both women looked up from their tape.

"Your Zach is a man of firm opinions," Mrs. Hargrove said with a smile for Jenny. "Charley says he has a fine bent for reasoning."

"He's not *my* Zach," Jenny said. She'd thought he would be. When he'd left her place on Christmas Day, she'd been filled with hope for their future. She thought he'd asked her to wait for him. But even if they were both waiting, shouldn't there be some communication?

Zach hadn't mentioned anything about *them* since Christmas Day, and it had been three weeks. Oh, he'd come by and fixed the roof during a thaw a week ago. And he'd towed her car into Dry Creek so Jasmine Hunter, the woman staying with Mrs. Hargrove, could repair everything that was wrong with it. Zach had even come by so the children could show him their new kittens. Andy particularly wanted to show him the two black kittens. He'd named one Lightning and the other Thunder.

But Jenny may as well have not even been there. The cowboy hadn't said one personal thing to her in all that time. Just because she was waiting for him didn't mean she didn't want to talk to him. She would rather he'd let the roof cave in and the car sit and rust instead of ignoring her. A man with intentions would at least be talking to the woman he was thinking about, wouldn't he?

"He's just trying to be sure," Mrs. Hargrove said softly.

Jenny grunted and looked down the length of the sanctuary to the closed door of the pastor's study. She wondered if Zach was trying to be sure about God or about her. Maybe he wasn't talking to her because he couldn't think of any kind way to tell her that he had changed his mind about her and was moving on.

Maybe he'd written to his showgirl friend and told her that he'd be coming to Vegas, after all. A showgirl had to be an easier romance than a widow with two small children. Zach could easily explain being late for Christmas since Thunder had been running a fever. Of course, the horse was fine now, but the showgirl probably didn't know anything about how long it would take a horse to recover from something like that.

Zach was going to break her family's heart, Jenny thought. The children had finally started to talk a little bit about their father. The night when they had told Zach that their father was gone had been a breakthrough for them. They were finally starting to heal, the way she'd hoped they would when she'd decided to move to Dry Creek.

Jenny felt a surge of anger toward Zach. Her children were going to start grieving all over again when Zach left. They'd miss him when he was gone as much as they missed their father, maybe more.

It wasn't fair. Zach had made their life worse, not better. She should have known he would, she told herself. He'd gotten their hopes up and now he was going to say goodbye.

On the other side of the closed door, Zach was straddling a wooden chair. Pastor Matthew was sitting at his desk, and Charley was sitting in the padded side chair.

Zach didn't agree with the pastor. He thought that the pastor and Charley both must have some of it wrong. Zach hadn't found out where they were wrong; his reading of the Bible hadn't got him to that part yet. But there had to be an exceptions clause. All contracts had them. He could show them the place in the Ranger cereal contracts where the exceptions were; he'd find the place in the Bible if he kept looking.

"But I used to cheat at cards," Zach was

saying. "And I was playing for money, not just matchsticks. Sometimes it was big money, too. No dimes or anything."

The curtains on the window were open and sunlight was spilling into the room. It was the middle of the morning, and Charley was shaking his head.

"I keep trying to tell you, but you won't listen," Charley finally said. "There are no exceptions. It doesn't matter if you'd gone out and murdered someone. If you confess the thing before God with repentance, you can still become a Christian."

"Who would I have murdered? Somebody who deserved it?"

"It doesn't matter," Charley said. "It could be anyone."

"Could it be you?"

"Well, technically, I suppose…" Charley sounded a little less sure.

"See, you wouldn't like it if someone murdered you and then you had to sit down next to them in heaven and be all buddy-buddy," Zach said firmly.

"Well, I might not like it, but I'd do it," Charley half shouted as he stood up. "That's what forgiveness is all about."

Zach stood up so he could meet his friend eye-to-eye.

The pastor cleared his throat. "Why don't we take a break and go get a cup of coffee? I have a whole pot in the kitchen."

Charley nodded. "Edith's out there measuring things. I should go check and see if she needs any help."

"I suppose Jenny Collins is helping her again," the pastor said.

Zach just swallowed. He had pledged to avoid Jenny, but it wasn't easy.

"That deal still on?" Zach asked Charley.

Charley nodded. He didn't even need to ask what deal Zach meant; the cowboy asked about it every day. "I've told all the single men that she needs more time. No one is to ask her out until the wedding. You'll all have the same chance with her."

"Is that after the ceremony, after the cake, or when the music first starts?" There was a pause as Zach studied the eyes turned his way. "What? Don't look at me like that. You both know that Max is ready to go. I wouldn't be surprised if some of the hands from the Elkton Ranch are coming to the wedding just to ask Jenny out, too. We need to have some clarification here, or someone's going to be talking to Jenny while Mrs. Hargrove walks down the aisle. I don't intend to let my chance get away just because I was waiting for the cake to be cut."

Charley chuckled. "I guess you're right. The second Edith is my wife, you men are welcome to take your best shot."

Zach nodded. "Be sure the rest of the guys know."

Charley shook his head. "Just don't ask her out until then. I won't have the guys saying I'm playing favorites."

"You've got my word."

The men were silent for a minute.

"Of course, it doesn't mean you can't sit and drink a cup of coffee together," Pastor Matthew said as he stood. "Just being friendly, you know. Since we all seem to be here together."

Zach suspected the pastor made a pot of coffee every time they met just so they'd have an excuse to ask Mrs. Hargrove and Jenny to join them. He wasn't sure how Mrs. Hargrove convinced Jenny to be there helping her measure something for the wedding every time he had his session, but the older woman had managed it.

It hadn't escaped Zach's notice that he had some friends in Dry Creek. And the feeling went both ways. The fact was, he'd have a hard time sitting down in heaven with anyone who had murdered someone in Dry Creek no matter what the Bible said on the matter. Not that Charley would want to hear that. It was coffee time.

"What are they measuring today?" Zach asked as he and Charley filed out of the pastor's office.

"Floral arrangements," Charley said. "I figure we need lots of floral arrangements. Edith loves the smell of roses."

"It'll cost you a fortune to fill the front of the church with roses," Zach said as the men walked to the kitchen.

"What price can you put on love?" Charley said with a grin.

Zach grunted as he accepted the cup of coffee the pastor held out to him. The funny thing was that Charley meant it, too. Zach figured the least he could do was to buy those roses for his friend. If anyone was going to go bankrupt because of love in Dry Creek, it ought to be him.

## Chapter Thirteen

Three months later Jenny stood in a Sunday-school room that had been converted into a woman's changing room for the wedding. Mrs. Hargrove had asked her to be a bridesmaid and Jenny had gladly said yes.

Jenny had thought she'd never willingly attend another wedding, not after her heartache with Stephen. And, yet, here she was dressed in a pink satin dress with puffy sleeves. Mrs. Hargrove's daughter, Doris June, was the maid of honor, and Jenny was the bridesmaid.

"You're sure Mrs. Brown can handle the kids?" Jenny turned and asked for the second time. The post mistress had looked delighted when the children showed up in their wedding clothes to sit with her, but a lot could happen while everyone was waiting for the bride to walk down the aisle.

"The pastor's wife will help her," Mrs. Hargrove said from behind the screen that had been put up. "She's had experience with twin boys."

"I just hope Andy keeps that cat in the box I gave him."

She hadn't discovered that Andy had brought one of his kittens with him until they were already at the church. Fortunately, the pastor had an old box they cut holes in so the cat could stay in there at Andy's feet. The kitten had started to meow pitifully when it couldn't smell Andy anymore, but it seemed content to be in the box next to him.

"I just hope I remember my vows," Mrs. Hargrove said as she stepped out from behind the screen. "The first time I got married, no one expected anyone to write their own vows."

Mrs. Hargrove was a radiant bride, Jenny thought as she watched the older woman smooth down the ivory satin of her dress. There were some beads around the neckline of the dress and fine netting over the sleeves. The woman's short gray hair was curled and held back a little with a pearl comb. She was wearing some lipstick in honor of the day.

"I wish I'd insisted on a veil," Mrs. Hargrove said as she reached up to pat her hair. "In my day, the bride always had a veil, and the thing covers a multitude of problems. What does a groom know about a veil, anyway?"

Jenny smiled. She knew Charley was the one who had not wanted any veils. He'd told Mrs. Hargrove that he wanted to see her face every second as she walked down the aisle. Jenny sighed. Charley was a man who understood romance.

"You won't worry about anything," Jenny told her friend. "Not when you see Charley waiting for you at the front of the church."

Mrs. Hargrove gave a little smile. "I guess you're right. He promised to prompt me, anyway, if I lose my place in those vows. Would you believe, the man has the whole wedding service memorized? He even knows what the pastor is going to say to us. Charley made him write it out."

"He just wants to remember everything," Jenny said. "Forever."

Jenny had to stop her thoughts right there. She refused to have sad thoughts on this wedding day. She also refused to be even the least bit envious of the happiness of her good friends. She had to admit though that she would remember this day forever, too, and it had nothing to do with Charley Nelson and Edith Hargrove's wedding.

She was afraid this might be the last day she'd see Zach. He was still having sessions with the pastor, but Zach had stood up in church three weeks ago and given a testimony that was so heartfelt it made half of the people listening pull out their handkerchiefs. The cowboy had made his peace with God.

Jenny had given thanks for Zach's decision. First, for the sake of his soul, of course. But also—and here she had tried to keep her excitement under control—because she'd really thought that once Zach was a Christian he would come to her and *at least* ask her out on a date. She half expected him to drive out to her place that afternoon after church and sweep her up in a knee-bending kiss. But he hadn't. He hadn't even stopped by to inquire about her health or the state of her roof.

After a week passed and Zach hadn't come near her, she decided she had been mistaken. Zach wasn't planning a future with her. He must only be staying in Dry Creek for the wedding. Charley had asked him to be a groomsman, and Zach clearly wanted to honor the older man who had become his friend.

Once he did that, though, he had no reason to stay in town.

Jenny knew that Mrs. Hargrove and Charley were doing their best to encourage a romance between her and Zach. She half suspected that the reason a bridesmaid and extra groomsman had been added to the wedding party was so that the two of them would be standing up there in front, getting a close up look at the wedding while standing across the aisle from each other.

It was probably supposed to be an inspiration to them.

There was a knock at the door to the room and someone called out, "It's time."

Mrs. Hargrove took a deep breath and picked up her rose bridal bouquet. "Here we go."

Jenny told herself just to concentrate on the roses. Their smell was the first thing she'd noticed when she'd come into the church earlier. That morning, a couple of floral trucks from Billings had delivered dozens of vases of red and pink roses. The whole front of the church looked like a garden. She'd asked Mrs. Hargrove about the roses, but the older woman only said that a friend of Charley's had sent them as a wedding gift.

At least one man knew how special wedding days were, Jenny thought as she stood beside the door leading into the back of the church. The pianist hadn't started yet, and Doris June was having some last words with her mother before they opened the door and all started down the aisle.

Zach stood at the front of the church next to Charley and Charley's son. They were waiting for the bride to appear, and Charley was nervous. Zach could tell because the older man kept reaching up to loosen his tie.

It was those tuxedoes, Zach thought in sympathy.

He hadn't worn a tuxedo in years. Usually, his dress clothes were a pressed western shirt and one of his championship belt buckles. Zach felt as uncomfortable in a tuxedo as he had in that old Santa suit. Not that he had anything against the red suit, he told himself with a smile. He'd managed to buy it from Mrs. Brown, and he'd only had to pay her twice what it would cost to buy a new one.

Fortunately, his bank account was healthy. He'd just signed another contract with the Ranger Flakes people and he had enough to set himself up raising horses. He hadn't picked out the land yet; he wanted to talk to Jenny first.

He had a lot he wanted to talk to Jenny about after Charley and Mrs. Hargrove were married.

The music started, and Zach felt his own mouth go dry. He hadn't been this nervous since the first time he'd stood at the corral chute getting ready to ride Black Demon. Back then, the worst that could happen would be breaking a bone or two. He had a feeling that before this day was over he could break his heart.

The doors at the back of the church opened, and there stood the women. Zach knew Mrs. Hargrove and her daughter, Doris June, were there, all shining in their satin dresses, but the only one he wanted to look at was Jenny.

Jenny was beautiful. She started walking down the aisle as the music played. She was carrying one of the smaller bouquets that Zach had bought to go along with the vases of roses. Her dress was pink and he swore she looked like a princess. Her face was flushed with excitement and her eyes fixed on— Zach stopped. Had Jenny just looked at Max Daniels?

Leave it to the rancher to sit so close to the front and to be so close to the edge of the pew. Anyone walking down the aisle would have to see Max, Zach told himself.

Of course, Zach told himself *he* was right in front of the church, and Jenny didn't seem to have any problem keeping her eyes off *him*.

Everyone in the church stood. Mrs. Hargrove

was beginning her walk down the aisle. Zach was worried Charley was going to stop breathing; the older man had drawn his breath in and had not let it out yet. He was staring at his bride. Zach was almost ready to go give the older man a quiet thump on the back when he heard the old man breath again.

Finally, the three women were standing at the front of the church with them and the guests were sitting down.

Then the pastor started to talk. Zach tried to listen, but he found he had a breathing problem of his own. Jenny was standing in front of the church with him and the pastor was talking about making a life-altering commitment. Granted, Jenny and he weren't the ones making the commitment, but Zach couldn't help but wonder if she was wondering what it would be like to have the pastor say those same words over them some day.

Jenny was focusing on the shoulder of Charley's tuxedo. She wasn't used to being up in front of people, and she had the strangest sensation that people were staring at her. They were supposed to be staring at the bride.

The pastor mentioned how important friendship was in a marriage and how the bride and groom had been friends for so long.

Jenny heard a ripple of movement among the guests and turned to look. Andy was standing at the back of the aisle with an empty box in his hands. Oh, dear. That kitten.

Someone in the third row gasped, and someone in the second row whispered, "Catch it."

Jenny looked back at the bride and groom. They didn't seem to have heard any of the sounds from the rest of the church. Hopefully, someone would catch the kitten and everything would be quiet again. Jenny motioned for Andy to go back to his seat, and she saw Mrs. Brown go to get him.

Then Jenny glanced down. The black kitten was curled up next to Zach's boots. The cat looked thoroughly content.

Mrs. Hargrove was repeating her vows, and Jenny watched her friend's face. The older woman didn't need any prompts as she promised to love her friend Charley for as long as she had left to live.

Jenny had to blink after Mrs. Hargrove finished her vows.

And then, all too soon, the pastor was pronouncing the older couple man and wife.

"Now you may kiss the bride," the pastor said. When Charley did just that, a cheer rose from among the guests. Everyone was smiling.

Charley and his bride were starting back

down the aisle. Then Doris June and her husband were walking down the aisle behind them. That left only Jenny and Zach standing.

Then Zach scooped up the black kitten and held out his arm to Jenny. She started walking with him. At least everyone had turned to watch the newly married couple so no one was watching her and Zach.

"Don't look," Zach hissed after they'd taken a step or two.

"Huh?" Jenny looked up at him. She wondered if the kitten had got away again, but it was curled up in the hand Zach had to his chest.

Even with the kitten in one hand, Zach pulled Jenny closer to him as they walked.

"I want to take you out to dinner," he whispered. By that time, they were almost at the back of the church.

"But there's the reception."

"Not now," Zach said. They'd finished their walk and were standing at the back of the church. "I mean later. I just want to ask you out on a date at your earliest convenience. I'm thinking tomorrow."

By now, everyone had left the aisle, and Jenny felt a tug on her dress.

"You found Thunder," Andy whispered as he looked over at Zach.

Zach handed down the kitten. "I think he missed you."

"He got lost," Andy agreed. "But you found him."

Zach gave a quick smile to the boy, but his eyes were on Jenny when he spoke. "He mostly found me."

Zach could see Max coming closer. And Jenny hadn't answered him.

"I know I'm not a perfect man," Zach said. "And I'm not exactly used to dating a woman like you."

"You have Patti," Jenny said.

Zach never was one to stay down when a horse threw him. "What I'm trying to say is that I'd like the chance to get to know you better."

"How much better?" Jenny asked.

Max was standing right beside them now. Zach closed his eyes. "I want to marry you."

"What?" Jenny asked.

"What?" Max bellowed. "I thought we were all supposed to have a fair turn at dating Jenny."

"What?" Jenny asked again.

It took several minutes for Jenny to begin to understand what the men were talking about. It only took one more second for her to face Zach. "You proposed to me to beat out Max, here?"

Zach shook his head. "I'm not very good with words."

Jenny looked at him in disbelief. "You've dated showgirls."

"But that's not like you and me. I didn't feel—" Zach's jaw was clenched, and he had that fierce look on his face again. "I just thought you should know where I'm headed, that's all. I know you can do better. But I've been meeting with the pastor to learn how to be a better family man."

Jenny touched his arm. "When?"

Zach looked at her blankly. "Thursdays. Same as usual."

"No, I mean when—"

For the first time, Zach noticed that Jenny's face was flushed. Max was still scowling and hovering, but Andy had given the man the kitten to hold so Zach decided the rancher would have to be content with that.

"When will we marry?" Zach asked softly.

Jenny nodded.

Zach felt a slow smile spread across his face. Almost everyone had left this part of the church and had gone down to the basement for the reception. He bent down and kissed Jenny.

Jenny felt the church tilt a little. She heard a growl and couldn't tell if it was the kitten or

Max. Then she didn't hear anything but her own heartbeat. Zach was kissing her. Then he kissed her again.

Zach broke away from the kiss and whispered in her ear. "I forgot to tell you that I love you. I meant to say that before."

Zach looked in her eyes and kissed her again.

Jenny heard purring. Someone really should do something about that kitten. Then she realized that Max, the kitten and Andy had all left. The sound must be coming from her heart.

\* \* \* \* \*

Dear Reader,

When Zach came into Dry Creek for the first time, he was a bitter man who was disillusioned with Christmas, God and himself. His best friend was a horse and the woman he was hoping to spend the holidays with didn't care if he showed up or not. Misery and loneliness are always more difficult on December 25.

One of the reasons I love to read and write Christmas stories is that everything seems more emotional on that day than at any other times of the year. We all have expectations of the day, whether they are good ones or bad. My expectations go more toward the cookies my mother used to bake when I was a child and the sounds of carols at church. There is a midnight Christmas Eve service that I love to go to each year. As I sit with friends and sing the timeless carols, I celebrate the birth of Jesus and feel connected to Christmas from generations past.

I do, however, have friends who have difficult childhood memories of Christmas and always just want to get through the day. I'm sure you have friends or family members who feel the same. Or perhaps you feel that way, too. One of the amazing things about God is that He loves us all the same—those who bound forward with joy and those who hang back in fear. We are all His on that day.

I wish you all kinds of joy this coming Christmas. I also love to hear from my readers at the holidays. If you get a chance, go to my Web site at www.JanetTronstad.com and send me an e-mail. If you don't have access to the Web, you can always drop me a note in care of the editors at Steeple Hill Books, 233 Broadway, Suite 1001, New York, NY 10279.

Wishing you a Merry Christmas.

*Janet Tronstad*

# QUESTIONS FOR DISCUSSION

1. Why does Zach Lucas hate Christmas? Have you ever felt the way he does about the holiday? Why or why not?

2. Zach talks about trying to make Christmas special for his family once when he was a boy and they didn't appreciate it. Do you feel that the effort it takes to make Christmas a special day is worth it? Why or why not?

3. At one point, Jenny feels she hasn't made Christmas special enough for her children. Have you ever felt that way? Do you think children have too many expectations of the holiday?

4. How do you make sure that Christ is the center of your holiday? Jenny always reads the Nativity story with her children; is there something else you do in your home?

5. Zach isn't the only one who is uncomfortable with family holidays. How can the church be made more sensitive to this fact?

6. When the family and Zach are snowbound, they have to make their own Christmas presents. Have you ever done that as a family? Do you think the holiday was more meaningful when people did make their own presents? Why or why not?

7. Jenny moves to Dry Creek, Montana, to start a new life for her children. Have you ever moved somewhere to start over? What was your experience? Did you find the new community welcoming?

8. Jenny wants to be able to take care of herself and her children in this new place. She needs the help of her neighbors, though. Have you ever felt the frustration of needing help when you wanted to be independent?

9. Jenny doesn't want anyone to know how empty her marriage was before her husband died. Why do you think this was? Have you ever been ashamed of something that was not your fault? Do you think Jenny blamed herself for the fact her husband did not want to spend time with his own family?

10. Jenny's son, Andy, wants Santa to bring him a cowboy for Christmas, but really wants a father. There are a lot of single parents these days. How can your church help them?

11. Zach is reluctant to tell Jenny how he feels because he thinks she had a wonderful marriage and believes he can't compete with her deceased husband. Have you ever been afraid to do something because you didn't think you would measure up?

12. Even after Zach comes back for Jenny, he knows he needs to spend some time figuring out his life before he will make a good husband. Do you agree that he needed to do that? Why or why not?

*Can't get enough of Dry Creek?*
*Make sure you see how it all began.*
*Look for*
*CALICO CHRISTMAS AT DRY CREEK*
*by Janet Tronstad. Available November 2009*
*from Steeple Hill Love Inspired Historical®*
*at your favorite retail outlet.*

*Fort Keogh, Montana Territory, 1879*

Elizabeth O'Brian heard voices outside her tent and thought it must be Mr. Miller coming to see if she was dead yet. It was a cold November day, and she'd been sitting in her tent for eleven days now in this desolate land. It had taken her husband, Matthew, and their baby only a few days to die from the fever, so Elizabeth couldn't fault the blacksmith for being impatient.

"Mrs. O'Brian," a man's voice called in the distance.

Elizabeth ignored the voice. Mr. Miller knew she was still waiting for the fever to come upon her. He would just have to be patient a little longer. It wasn't as easy to die as it looked.

"Mrs. O'Brian," the same man's voice called out. He was closer now.

She frowned. It didn't sound like Mr. Miller calling her.

Elizabeth got her knees and crawled to the opening of the tent, She saw two men standing a proper distance away.

She could see Sergeant Rawlings plainly, but the other man had his back to her. Initially she thought he was one of the soldiers form the fort, too. But when she looked at him more closely, she realized he couldn't be a soldier. He wore a buckskin jacket and he had a black fur of some kind wrapped around his shoulders in a sling.

She shivered, and this time it was not from the cold. He must be an Indian.

It wasn't until the man in the buckskin jacket moved that Elizabeth saw the Indian girl sitting on the pinto pony near the fort. She must be about nine or ten years old, and she had a blanket wrapped around her. Elizabeth couldn't imagine why the girl was watching them so intently.

"Could you just come out here, please?" Sergeant Rawlings called out again.

Really—men, Elizabeth thought to herself. She supposed it never occurred to any of them to let her die in peace. Elizabeth wrapped a blanket around her like a shawl and stepped out of the tent. She had taken several steps when the man in the buckskin turned around and she saw him fully for the first time.

She stopped and stared. Why, he wasn't an Indian at all. His eyes were blue, and the skin around his eyes, the part that was wrinkled from squinting, was undeniably white. Up close, he seemed larger than she expected. And more fierce than a white man should be. He looked like a warrior, no matter what color he was.

She was still staring at the other man. She'd never had this kind of breathless reaction to the sight of anyone. Of course, it probably wasn't really the sight of this that was causing her heart to continue racing. It was only that she had thought he was a savage capable of doing Gold only knew what.

Even now that Elizabeth knew the man she was looking at was a white man, she was still uneasy around him. He was nothing at all like Matthew. Nothing like any man she'd ever seen before.

Oh, dear—whatever he was, he was looking straight at her and frowning.

Then he spoke. "There must be some mistake. She doesn't look like a widow—just look at her."

"Please don't let me appearance concern you. I normally do better," she said.

"I never said there was anything wrong with the way you look." The man's eyes softened. "I just expected someone older. And not so pretty."

Elizabeth watched in horror as the man reached out and touched her chin as if she was a child to be consoled.

"I'm hardly pretty," Elizabeth said, a little more sharply than she intended. She moved her face slightly to discourage him, although his touch on her chin had been gentle and surprisingly pleasant.

"Well, I can't expect you to help me," the buckskin man finally said before turning to the sergeant as if he hadn't just been smiling at her.

"There's nobody else. You've got to ask her—for the baby's sake."

"What…" Elizabeth looked around. "What baby?"

She saw the buckskin man's hand go to the bundle he wore across his chest.

"This baby," the man said.

"Ohhh. Can I see it?"

The man started to turn the bundle toward her.

"Where's her mother?"

"Dead," the man said flatly, and then "The doctor says you're not going to get the fever." He looked square at her. "You're her last hope. She'll die without something to eat."

Elizabeth nodded. "Of course, I—I will do what I can until some other way is found."

"What other way is there?" the man asked. His voice was strained, too. "You are our only hope."

# *Love Inspired*®
# SUSPENSE
## RIVETING INSPIRATIONAL ROMANCE

Watch for our new series of
edge-of-your-seat suspense novels.
These contemporary tales
of intrigue and romance
feature Christian characters
facing challenges to their faith...
and their lives!

Steeple
Hill®

Visit:
**www.SteepleHill.com**

LISUSDIR07R

*Love Inspired.*
# HISTORICAL
### INSPIRATIONAL HISTORICAL ROMANCE

Engaging stories of romance,
adventure and faith,
these novels are set in
various historical periods
from biblical times
to World War II.

## NOW AVAILABLE!

Steeple
Hill®

For exciting stories that reflect traditional values,
visit:
**www.SteepleHill.com**